Tales *from the* Brothers Grimm *and the* Sisters Weird

YEARLING BOOKS are designed especially to entertain and enlighten young people. Patricia Reilly Giff, consultant to this series, received her bachelor's degree from Marymount College and a master's degree in history from St. John's University. She holds a Professional Diploma in Reading and a Doctorate of Humane Letters from Hofstra University. She was a teacher and reading consultant for many years, and is the author of numerous books for young readers.

Tales *from the* Brothers Grimm *and the* Sisters Weird

Vivian Vande Velde

A YEARLING BOOK

Published by
Bantam Doubleday Dell Books for Young Readers
a division of
Bantam Doubleday Dell Publishing Group, Inc.
1540 Broadway
New York, New York 10036

ISBN: 0-440-41300-1

Reprinted by arrangement with Harcourt Brace & Company

Printed in the United States of America

June 1997

10 9 8 7 6 5 4 3

CWO

To the children of the Rochester area schools,
who have provided me with lots
of ideas for stories,
and especially to the children of
Twelve Corners School,
who provided me with this one.

And to Cynthia "Wild Washerwoman" DeFelice,
who came up with the right answer before
I even knew there was a question.

Contents

Tales *from the* Brothers Grimm *and the* Sisters Weird

Straw into Gold

Once upon a time, in the days before Social Security or insurance companies, there lived a miller and his daughter, Della, who were fairly well-off and reasonably happy until the day their mill burned down.

Suddenly they had nothing except the clothes they were wearing: no money, nor any way to make money, nor any possibility of ever getting money again unless they came up with a plan.

Now the miller was very good at milling, and he was fairly good at being a father, but at planning he was no good at all.

His plan was this: They would sit by the side of the road and wait for someone who looked rich to pass by. Then the miller would announce: "My daughter can spin straw into gold. If you give us three gold pieces, she will spin a whole barnful of straw into gold for you." If the rich people were interested — and the miller pointed out that they couldn't help but be interested — he would then say that his daughter's magic only worked by moonlight. "You must leave her alone — completely undisturbed — all night long. And by dawn all of the straw will be spun into gold."

"I don't understand this plan," Della said. "I'm not very good at spinning, even wool, and I have no idea how — "

"No, no," the miller interrupted, "you don't understand."

"That's what I just said." Della sighed.

"Listen," the miller explained, "the plan, of course, is for the two of us to take our fee of three gold pieces and run away during the night."

"That's dishonest," Della pointed out.

"So it is," her father admitted. "But we will

take those three gold pieces and rebuild our mill. Once the mill is working again, we will save all our money until we can repay the people we've tricked."

Della still didn't like this plan, but since she herself had no experience beyond milling and being a daughter, she agreed.

So Della and her father sat by the side of the road, and the first rich person to pass by was the richest person in the land: he was the king.

"Oh, dear," Della said, recognizing the royal crest on the door of the carriage, "maybe we should wait—"

But if the miller was not good at making plans, he was even worse at changing plans once they were made. Standing in the middle of the road, he called out, "My daughter can spin straw into gold. If you give us three gold pieces, she will spin a whole barnful of straw into gold for you."

The king motioned for the driver to stop the horses. "You," he said, leaning out of the window. "Both of you, come closer." The king had clothes of red satin and brocade, sewn with gold thread. He wore more rings than he had fingers, and he had a dark wig, which was all thick ringlets around his pale face. He put a silk handkerchief to his nose, for Della and her father still smelled of smoke from their burned-down mill. "What did you say?" he demanded.

The miller wasn't sure if this question meant the king was interested and he should now explain about the moonlight and the being left alone, or if it meant the king was slightly deaf and hadn't heard the first part. The miller decided he'd better repeat himself. He raised his voice and enunciated clearly. "My daughter can spin straw into gold. If you give us three gold pieces, she will spin a whole barnful of straw into gold for you."

"If she can spin straw into gold," the king asked, "then why are the two of you dressed in filthy rags?"

"Ah," the miller said. "Well . . ." Once again he had been all prepared to explain about the moonlight and the being left alone, and now that he couldn't say that, he had no idea what to say. "Why are we dressed in rags?" he repeated. "That's a very good question. That's an excellent question."

The king dabbed at his nose, then let his handkerchief drop into the mud by the road, since he only ever used a handkerchief once. He pulled out a new one.

"Our mill burned down," Della explained.

"Yes," the miller agreed. "Including the spinning wheel. And the straw."

"Hmmm," the king said. "Very well. You may follow the carriage to the castle. You will be provided with your three gold pieces, a spinning wheel, and straw." He dropped his second handkerchief without having used it at all and motioned for the driver to get the horses moving.

The miller nudged his daughter as they started down the road after the carriage. "See," he said. "I told you the plan would work."

"Yes," Della said, "so you did." But she was still worried.

And rightly so. For when they got to the castle, the plan began to fall apart.

The king insisted that Della work at her spinning in the castle itself instead of in the barn.

"But," the miller protested, "she needs to work her magic at night, by the light of the moon."

"Fine," the king said. "The rooms on the second floor have windows to let in the moonlight."

The miller gulped, since it would be harder to get Della away if she was up on the second floor. He tried again. "But if anybody interrupts Della while she's working her magic, then the magic will reverse itself and all the gold she's spun will turn back into straw."

"We'll lock her in the room to make sure nobody interrupts her," the king said.

Della gave her father a warning nudge before he could say anything else to make matters even worse.

"And of course," the king said, "if she fails to spin this straw into gold, I will have her head chopped off." To the servants he said, "Lock this man away for the night so he doesn't try to escape." As two of the largest servants took the miller by the arms, the king told him, "Come back tomorrow, and I will give you your three gold pieces or your daughter's head."

"But . . . but . . ." the miller started, but before he could think of anything to say, he was dragged out of the room.

Leaving Della, for the first time in her life, on her own.

The king had her led up to a room that was as big as the entire mill had been. Servants brought in a spinning wheel, and then load after load after load after load of straw until the whole room was filled with straw, except for the area around the spinning wheel.

How am I ever going to get out of this? Della thought. She hoped to slip out of the room while the servants were making their deliveries, but someone was always watching her. Then, after the king's guards locked her in, she tried to get the door open with her hairpin, the way heroines in stories always do, but in the end all she had was a bent hairpin. She couldn't even climb out the window, which was too narrow to pass through and very high up. And even if she did get out — what about her father?

She kicked the spinning wheel, which made her feel a little bit better but not much.

The servants hadn't even given her anything to eat, and now as the room got darker and darker until the only light was the moonlight coming through her prison window, Della added dinner to the list of meals she'd missed that day.

Sitting on the hard floor, the last thing in the world she intended to do was to start crying, but that's exactly what she did.

After a while — after a long while — she used her sleeve to rub her eyes and nose since she didn't have a handkerchief, silk or otherwise. From behind her came the sound of someone clearing his throat discreetly. Out of the corner of her eye, Della saw that whoever was behind her was offering her a handkerchief.

Without turning around, Della tried to work out exactly what she would say. "You see," she started, "actually crying is necessary for the magic. . . . Tears, tears are the lubricant for the spinning wheel . . . but it only works if I'm totally alone, and since you were watching, I won't be able to do the spell again until — " At this point, she did turn around, and she stopped talking midexplanation.

She'd been expecting to see the king or one of his servants. Instead, crouched beside her was a young man who was obviously not even human. In fact, he was an elf. Tall and slender, with pointy ears, he'd been listening very attentively if somewhat quizzically.

"Well, that doesn't make a lot of sense," he told her, but then he smiled, and she saw he was handsome in a strange, otherworldly way. He added, "But I do admire your quick thinking."

"Who are you?" Della gasped in surprise. "What do you want? How did you get in here?"

The young elf paused a moment to consider, then answered in the order she'd asked: "Rumpelstiltzkin. I heard you crying and came to see what was the matter. Sideways between the particles."

"What?" Della asked.

The elf raised his voice slightly. "Rumpelstiltzkin. I heard you crying and — "

"No," Della said, "I mean . . . *sideways?*"

Rumpelstiltzkin nodded. "The world of humans and the world of magic exist side by side." He illustrated by holding his hands out, his long, slender fingers spread, then he put his hands together, intertwining his fingers. "So that we're taking up the space that you're not" — he was watching her skeptically as if suspecting that she wasn't getting this, which she wasn't — "and vice versa."

"Oh," she said. "And you heard me crying from your world?"

"Well," the young elf said gently, "you were crying quite loudly."

Della finally took the handkerchief he was offering and wiped her nose. Blowing would have been more effective, she knew, but too noisy and undignified. "I don't usually cry. I know it's stupid and it doesn't help anything and it's unattractive and—"

"And I heard it," Rumpelstiltzkin said. "And I came to see what was the matter. So sometimes it *does* help." He stood and looked around the room. "Castle," he said as though he hadn't noticed before where he was. "Despite the straw." He looked more closely at Della. "You don't look like a castle person."

"I'm not," she admitted. "I'm a mill person. Except that our mill burned down. And my father told the king I could spin straw into gold so that we could get a little bit of gold from the king so that we could rebuild the mill and then we would have paid the gold back except that the king locked my father in the dungeon and me in here and I have to spin all this straw into gold tonight or he's going to cut off my head."

Rumpelstiltzkin was obviously impressed. "You can spin straw into gold?"

"No," Della said.

"Then," Rumpelstiltzkin said, "I think your plan has a flaw."

"That's why I was crying." Della rested her face in her hands.

"You're not going to start crying again, are

you?" Rumpelstiltzkin asked, sounding worried.

"No," Della said. "You can go back where you came from. I won't bother you again."

But the young elf stayed where he was.

After a while he said, "You weren't *bothering* me. I just wish I could help you."

The sad thing was that, even without raising her head and looking at him, Della could tell he was sincere. Helpless, but sincere.

"I think it's really sweet," he continued, "that you were planning to return the money even before the king gave it to you. But I've never heard of spinning straw into gold. I wouldn't know where to begin."

"That's all right," Della said. "Probably getting one's head chopped off is less unpleasant than starving to death."

After another while Rumpelstiltzkin said, "But I do have another idea."

Della finally looked up.

"We could throw the straw out the window, then I could replace it with gold from my world, so long as it doesn't have to be spun out."

"I'm sure the king wouldn't complain no matter what form the gold was in, but would you really be willing to do that?"

Rumpelstiltzkin nodded. "In exchange."

"In exchange for what?" Della asked.

"What do you have?"

Della considered. The mill had burned down. All she had was what she'd been wearing when the fire had started: her second-best dress with her mother's wedding ring pinned to the collar for decoration. "I have this gold ring, which belonged to my mother before she died," Della said, unpinning the ring and holding it out.

Rumpelstiltzkin looked from her to the ring back to her again. "You want me to substitute this straw for a roomful of gold, and you're offering me one gold ring in exchange?"

Della felt her face go red in embarrassment. "I'm sorry," she said. "I wasn't thinking—"

"No, no," Rumpelstiltzkin said. "I didn't mean . . ." She could tell he was genuinely distressed he'd embarrassed her. "The ring will be fine."

She handed it over, for even if he meant to take it and run and never come back with gold for the straw, she wouldn't be any worse off than she was now.

But he didn't run off. He kept disappearing (sideways, he insisted, between the particles), but he kept returning with gold cups and gold coins and gold jewelry, assuring her that everything would be fine, that the king couldn't possibly chop off her head. And Della kept throwing straw out the window, till the next thing she knew, she heard the king's voice on the other side of the door saying, "It's dawn. Unlock the door." She threw the last armful of straw out the window, and when she turned back, Rumpelstiltzkin was gone and the king was standing in the doorway, blinking in amazement.

"Well done," the king said, taking a bit of snuff. "I must say: well done."

"Thank you, sir," Della said, curtsying. "Now if you don't mind, sir . . ."

Before she could finish, the king gestured to one of the pages, who reached into a bag hanging from his belt. He picked out three gold coins and dropped them, one by one, into Della's hand.

"Thank you, sir," Della said, curtsying again. "I—"

"In fact," the king said, "this is so well done, I think we'll hire you again for tonight."

"Oh," Della said, "but—"

The king gestured to another page. "Clean her up," he ordered. "Feed her. Keep her amused till tonight." He looked around the room appreciatively again. "Well done," he repeated.

Which didn't make Della feel any better at all.

The servants dressed Della in a gown richer than any she'd ever had. And they laid out a banquet for her, the most delicious food she'd ever tasted, on silver dishes. And all day long different ones played the lute and sang songs for her, and they brushed her hair till it shone like silk, and they manicured her nails and were friendly in every way. But when evening came, they locked her in a room even bigger than the first and filled, except for the area around the spinning wheel, with straw.

Della sat down on the floor. *Well,* she told herself, *except for the threat of getting your head chopped off, you've never had a more wonderful day.* Then she tried to tell herself that she was lucky to have had the day, but she didn't feel lucky. All that gold Rumpelstiltzkin had brought, and here she was back where she had started. It was kind of him to have tried to help, but it was all for nothing. She put her face in her hands and sighed.

And looked up again when she felt a gentle touch on her arm. "I wasn't crying," she pointed out.

"No," Rumpelstiltzkin said, "but this time I was looking for you." He walked around the room, or at least that part of the room that wasn't filled with straw. "More straw into gold," he observed. "Is the king still threatening to cut off your head?"

Della nodded.

"Did he even pay you for the last batch?"

Della held out the three gold coins the king's page had given her.

"Quite a bargain." Rumpelstiltzkin crouched down beside her. "Offer them to me, and I'll bring more gold."

"Offer you three gold coins for a roomful of gold?" Della said. "At least the ring had sentimental value."

Rumpelstiltzkin just smiled at her. "Offer them to me," he repeated.

Della put the gold coins into his hand.

Then, just as they had done the previous night, Rumpelstiltzkin brought armloads of gold from between the particles while Della threw straw out the window. But this time Della knew the king would be pleased, so, instead of worrying, she and Rumpelstiltzkin talked and laughed together as though they were old friends.

By the time the king returned at dawn, all the straw was gone and the room was filled with gold.

"Thank you," Della whispered as they heard the key turn in the lock.

Rumpelstiltzkin bowed, then disappeared.

The door banged open.

"Well done!" the king exclaimed once again. "Truly, magnificently well done."

"Yes," Della said. "And now I must be leaving or my father will be wor—"

"Nonsense," the king said. "Your father is fine. And we're having such a good time together. I insist you stay."

"Stay?" Della repeated.

"Of course," the king said. "Someone with your abilities will make an excellent queen."

"Queen?" Della repeated.

The king gave a gracious nod. "Spin another roomful of straw into gold, and we'll consider it your dowry. I'll marry you the following day."

"Oh my," Della said.

The king gestured to one of the servants. "Dress her in the finest silks and jewels," he ordered. "Feed her off my own dishes. Treat her like a queen till tonight."

"But," Della started, "but—"

The king kissed her hand and swept out of the room.

The servants dressed Della in a gown richer than any she'd ever seen, heavy with beads and jewels, and there were more jewels for around her neck and fingers and to hang from her ears; and they laid out a banquet for her, with food even more sumptuous than the day before, and they served it on dishes of ivory, with knives and spoons of gold; and all day long they played violins and harpsichords for her; and they brushed her hair till it shone like gold, and pedicured her nails, and were respectful in every way. But when evening came, they locked her in a room even bigger than the first two rooms and filled, except for the area around the spinning wheel, with straw.

"Rumpelstiltzkin," Della said out loud, "if ever there was a time I needed you, now is it."

The young elf appeared before her. He bowed just as he'd been bowing when he'd disappeared that morning, as though he'd been waiting all day to come back to her.

"This time," Della said, "at least I have something to offer you." Taking off the ruby earrings, she said, "And I've thought of a way out of this:

I'll tell the king that my magic spinning cannot be done more than three times for any one person. Three is a magical number, you know." She unfastened the diamond necklace, but Rumpelstiltzkin hadn't even taken the earrings yet. "What's the matter?" she asked.

"Those aren't yours to give," he said. "Those are the king's."

"Oh." Della indicated her rings, and the jewels sewn into the bodice of her dress.

Rumpelstiltzkin shook his head. "Didn't the king pay you for the second roomful of gold?"

"No," Della said. "He told me he would marry me and make me queen."

"I see," Rumpelstiltzkin said. "First he says, 'Spin the straw into gold, or I'll chop your head off,' then he says, 'Spin the straw into gold, or I'll chop your head off,' then he says, 'Spin the straw into gold, and I'll marry you.' The man has a way with words. No wonder you want to marry him."

"That's not fair," Della protested. "It's not every day a miller's daughter gets the chance to marry a king."

"No," Rumpelstiltzkin said softly. "I would imagine not."

Della shivered. Having come so far, she had

finally let herself think that she might actually survive her father's plan. She said, "I have nothing to offer you."

Rumpelstiltzkin looked at her for a long moment before answering. "Then," he said, "I will do it for you for nothing."

Once again they worked together, Rumpelstiltzkin bringing gold from his world into the locked room while Della threw straw out the window. But while the first night they had worked frantically, unsure whether the king would be fooled, and while the second night they had worked enjoying each other's company—this third night they had nothing to say to each other, and they worked silently and grimly.

As Della threw the last handfuls of straw out the window, she turned to the young elf who had three times now saved her life and said, "Rumpelstiltzkin, I—"

But he had already returned to his own world without a word, leaving Della to wait for the king alone in the graying dawn.

The king was delighted with his new roomful of gold, but when Della told him that the laws of magic prohibited her from spinning any more gold for him, he complained bitterly that she had tricked him. He was all for chopping her head off, but the king's advisors said that, since the royal marriage had already been announced, this would probably be a bad idea.

And so the king and the miller's daughter were married.

The king decreed that, as queen, Della was prohibited from doing common things such as spinning, and he used this as an excuse for why she no longer spun straw into gold. And as for the miller, the king pronounced him Master Miller of the Realm, and all the other millers had to pay a tax to support him so that the king's father-in-law wouldn't have to support himself by common labor either.

But the king begrudged the gold Della no longer spun, and the marriage was not a happy one.

Eventually Della announced that she was expecting a child. This made the king happy, for he said it was time he had an heir. But when the child was born, it was a girl, and the king, saying a girl did not make a fit heir, wouldn't even visit his new daughter.

"Name her what you will," the king told Della. "It's no concern of mine."

Della sat on the window ledge of the nursery and rocked her unnamed baby daughter back and forth, so furious her eyes filled with angry tears. She stared out the window, so her tears wouldn't fall on the infant, for she was determined that the child should never learn how her own father did not love her.

From beside her, a soft voice said, "She's lovely," and Della turned and saw Rumpelstiltzkin gently touch the baby's tiny hand. "She's lovely," Rumpelstiltzkin repeated. "She looks just like you. Why are you crying?"

It was the first time Della had seen him in over a year, since that last morning in that roomful of gold. She wanted to tell him how very pleased she was to see him, how she had thought of his kindness every day of her queenship, but instead she blurted out how the king was disappointed to have a daughter instead of a son.

"Anyone with any sense would be proud to have her as a daughter," Rumpelstiltzkin said. "But maybe you could tell the king that when she gets to be older she'll be able to spin straw into gold." He knelt beside her. "I'll come back," he promised, "and bring him three more roomsful."

"That's very kind of you," Della said. "But I'm

sure he'd love her if he only stopped to think about it."

In a very quiet voice Rumpelstiltzkin said, "I don't think love is something you stop to think about."

"What I mean is," Della said, "I'm sure he *does* love her, but he just doesn't realize it. Maybe I should tell him she's sick. If he's worried about her, then he'll see how precious she is."

"But the servants would tell him she isn't sick," Rumpelstiltzkin pointed out. "You could tell him a wicked old elf is going to steal her away unless . . ."

Rumpelstiltzkin paused to consider, and Della said, "You don't look wicked or old."

Rumpelstiltzkin smiled at her, which made him look even less wicked and old.

It almost made Della wish . . . But that was too dangerous a thought.

"We'll tell him that you're the one who taught me how to spin straw into gold," she said. "And that in exchange I promised you my firstborn child. The only way to break the agreement . . ." She sighed. "Whatever you ask the king to do," she said, "it has to be something easy to make sure he can do it."

"Certainly," Rumpelstiltzkin agreed. "How easy?"

Della thought and finally said, "He has to guess your name."

"Easier," Rumpelstiltzkin suggested. "It's not that common a name."

"Tell him you'll give him three days before you'll take the baby," Della said. "Surely in that time we can arrange some way for somebody to learn your name."

But it wasn't as easy as Della thought.

The king was too busy with councils and court decisions to even ask why a wicked old elf wanted his daughter. But he did have the servants in the castle write out a list of all the names they could think of.

The next day, when Rumpelstiltzkin appeared in the throne room, the king read out every name they had, starting with Aaron and ending with Zachary.

Rumpelstiltzkin shook his head after each name, and when it was over he said they had two more days but they'd never guess.

The king had to be at the dedication of a new ship that day, but he ordered the councillors and scholars of the castle to look through all the old history chronicles and put together a list of every name they could find.

The next day, Rumpelstiltzkin again appeared in the throne room, and the king read out this new list, starting with Absolom and ending with Ziv.

Once again Rumpelstiltzkin shook his head after each name, but this time he gave Della a worried look before announcing they had one more day but they'd never guess. He was beginning to worry, Della could tell, that they never would.

The king had been invited to a hunting party with the neighboring king, but before leaving he sent servants out of the castle into the countryside to see if they could discover any new names.

As the servants trickled back home that night and the next morning, one after another with no new names, Della decided that she would have to just blurt out the name Rumpelstiltzkin and hope that the king didn't ask where she'd heard it.

Then the last of the castle servants returned.

"Good news, your majesty," this last man said to her. "Although I searched all day yesterday without finding any new names, as I was walking through the woods on the way back to the castle this morning, I came across that same elf who's been threatening the young princess. Fortunately he didn't see me. And even more fortunately he was dancing around a campfire singing, 'Yo-ho, Rumbleskilstin —' "

"Excuse me?" Della said. *Rumbleskilstin?*"

The servant repeated it, incorrectly again, saying, "He sang, 'Yo-ho, Rumbleskilstin is my name. Rumbleskilstin, Rumbleskilstin, Rumbleskilstin. The king doesn't know it. The queen doesn't know it. Only I know it, and I'm Rumbleskilstin.' "

"That's quite a song," Della said, trying not to laugh at the picture of the normally dignified Rumpelstiltzkin dancing around a campfire, and — after all that — the servant getting the name wrong. Still, Rumpelstiltzkin certainly wouldn't complain that it wasn't exactly right. "Well," she agreed, "this is indeed fortunate. You have our gratitude, mine and the king's."

At least Della hoped the king would be grateful.

Rumpelstiltzkin appeared in the throne room at the appointed time, but the king was late getting back from an appointment with the royal wigmaker. When the king did come in, laughing and chatting with his companions, he didn't appear nearly as worried as Rumpelstiltzkin did.

"We discovered a likely name," Della told the king.

"Good," he said, fluffing his new wig, which was even curlier than his other 150 wigs.

Look at me, Della thought at him furiously. *Look at your daughter.*

But the king looked, instead, at his reflection in the mirror and blew kisses to himself.

Hugging the baby close, Della turned to Rumpelstiltzkin, who *was* looking at them. *No one can change straw into gold,* Della thought to herself. *Some things are just straw, and some things are gold, and sometimes you just have to know which is which.*

She walked past the king to put her hand on Rumpelstiltzkin's arm, looked up into the young elf's eyes, and said, "Take us with you."

So Rumpelstiltzkin put his arm around her and stepped sideways, as always, between the particles.

The king, of course, hired his own messengers to spread the news of what had happened. But as for Rumpelstiltzkin and Della, they lived happily ever after. And it was Rumpelstiltzkin who chose the name for Della's baby girl. He called her Abigail, which means "a father's joy."

TWO

Frog

Once upon a time when princes still set out to seek their fortunes and when cranky old women still sometimes turned out to be witches, a prince named Sidney came to a well where an old woman asked him for help in getting water.

Now the old woman didn't have a bucket and Sidney didn't have a bucket. But he'd heard enough fairy tales about three sons setting off down the road and meeting a strange old woman, and the first two sons were always rude and got into trouble, and the youngest son was always polite and then the old woman would give him whatever it was that he needed to fulfill his quest. So — being a middle son — Sidney always did his best to be polite to everybody, even when he wasn't on a quest.

But his best wasn't enough for this old woman, and the next thing he knew he was a bulgy-eyed green frog, which just goes to show that sometimes having a bucket is more important than being polite.

"There, you loathsome thing," the old woman said, which was hardly fair since she was the one who had made him into what he was, "stay a frog until a beautiful princess feeds you from her plate and lets you sleep on her pillow."

Travel goes a lot faster when you're riding a horse than when you're hopping, especially if your feet are less than a foot long. It took several days for Sidney to find the nearest castle, and when he got there, he didn't even know whose castle it was. Everything looked different from grass level, but he was still pretty sure he didn't know the people who lived here. He hoped there was a princess.

Sidney hopped across the drawbridge and into the dusty courtyard. There were horses and dogs and chickens. People, too, way, way high up. And lots and lots of legs. Many of them were walking so fast that he knew he was in danger of getting stepped on. He saw a well in the courtyard, but Sidney had had quite enough of wells for the time being. Hurriedly, he hopped off to the side, where there was a quiet and well-tended garden.

In the garden was a lovely, cool-looking reflecting pool, with fresh, clear water and lily pads. Sidney jumped in and it felt like heaven.

Until something bonked him on the head and dunked him.

Sidney came up sputtering, just as a beautiful girl of about his own age came running up to the pool.

"Oh, no!" the girl cried. "My golden ball."

"Excuse me," Sidney said, "are you a princess?"

The girl didn't answer. She just flung herself onto the bench by the pool's edge and began to weep.

Sidney, in the middle of the pool, looked down and could see the ball just settling into the soft mud below him. He paddled closer to the girl.

"Excuse me," he said again, "are you a princess?"

"What a twit," the girl snapped, never even looking up. "Of course I am. Don't I look like one?"

"Yes, you do," Sidney admitted apologetically. "And a very lovely one at that. I think the two of us can help each other out."

"I don't want to help you out," the princess said. "I want to have my ball back."

"That's what I mean," Sidney said.

The princess finally looked at him. "You can get my ball?" she asked.

Sidney nodded.

"Well, then, do it."

"Yes," Sidney said, "but then, afterward, will you let me eat from your plate and sleep on your pillow? I'm a prince, you see, and I have a magic spell on me, and that's the only way to break it."

The princess's lip curled in disgust. "I need that ball. It's my father's paperweight and I wasn't supposed to be playing with it."

"I don't have to eat a *lot* from your plate," Sidney told her, "and I can sleep *way over* on the side of the pillow and not take up much room at all."

"Oh, all right," the princess said.

Sidney dove into the water. The ball was heavy, but with a great deal of struggling he finally managed to get it up close enough that the princess could reach over and grasp it. As she turned the ball over in her hands to make sure it wasn't damaged, Sidney jumped up onto the bench next to her. "Now," he said just as she shook the water off the ball, drenching him all over again. He coughed a little bit, and when he looked up again, she was gone.

"Wait," he called, catching sight of her leaving the garden.

But she didn't.

By the time he made it out of the garden, across the courtyard, and into the castle, the princess was sitting down to dinner with her family.

Sidney kicked on the dining-room door. "Hey," he yelled. "Hey, princess!"

He heard the king ask, "What's that noise?"

"Nothing," the princess answered.

"Princess!" Sidney yelled. "It's me, the frog prince. You accidentally left me behind."

The king's voice said, "He says he's a frog prince. What does he mean, you left him behind?"

"I don't know," the princess said.

"You promised you'd help me." Sidney wasn't used to yelling, and his throat was getting sore.

"You promised you'd help him?" the king asked.

"No," the princess said.

There was no other way. Sidney called out, "In return for getting back your father's golden ball paperweight that you were playing with and dropped into the pool in the garden."

"The golden paperweight that left a wet spot on my papers this afternoon?" the king asked.

"I don't know anything about it," the princess said.

The king must have brought his fist down on the table. Sidney could hear the dishes rattle. "A promise," the king said, "is a promise. Let the frog in."

Servants came and opened the big golden doors.

Sidney hopped into the dining room, which was decorated with mirrors and crystal chandeliers and hundreds of flickering candles. He hopped until he came to the princess's chair.

"What, exactly," the king asked his daughter, "did you promise him?"

"I can't remember," the princess said.

"That I could eat from your plate," Sidney reminded her. "That I could sleep on your pillow. *I* promised not to eat too much and to use only the corner of the pillow."

"A promise is a promise," the king repeated.

The princess lifted Sidney, not very gently, and plunked him down on the white linen tablecloth beside her china dish.

Sidney nibbled on a piece of lettuce that was hanging off the edge of the dish.

The princess put her napkin up to her mouth and made gagging sounds. "I'm all finished," she announced, shoving the plate away.

"Then you may leave the table," the king said. "Don't forget your little friend."

The princess scooped up Sidney and brought him up the stairs to her bedroom, stamping her feet all the way.

"Thank you," Sidney yelled back down the stairs to the king.

"You horrid beast," the princess growled at Sidney. "You told him about the paperweight. Now I'm going to be in trouble."

"It was your own fault for walking away so fast that I couldn't keep up," Sidney said.

"Are you going to put me on your pillow now?"

"I'll put you on my pillow!" the princess shouted. "But I'll put you on my wall first."

She flung Sidney with all her might against the wall.

"Ow!" Sidney cried, landing in a heap on the floor.

"Now here's the pillow," the princess said, throwing that on top of him.

But as soon as the pillow touched Sidney's head, he instantly regained his normal shape.

"Oh my!" the princess gasped. She was going to be in serious trouble with her father now, she thought. Here she had a man in her room and her father was never going to believe that this was the same person who had come into her room as a frog. Even now she could hear her father coming up the stairs, demanding, "What's all the commotion?"

But the prince — he was obviously a prince — who stood before her was incredibly handsome, and she was falling in love already, which surely would balance out the trouble she'd be in with her father.

"Oh," she said, clapping her hands together. "I'm so sorry. But my father will make it worth your while. We can get married, and he'll give you half the kingdom and — "

"Are you out of your mind?" Sidney said. "First you break your promise to me, then you lie about it until your father forces you to keep it, then you try to kill me. No, thank you, princess." He strode out of the door, out of the castle, out of the kingdom, returning home, where he eventually married the goose girl.

And the princess was right: her father didn't believe her story.

All Points Bulletin

All officers in the vicinity:
Be on the lookout for suspect
wanted for breaking and entry.
Stole the victims' food,
vandalized their furniture
from room to room.
May be armed;
may be dangerous.
Last known alias: Goldilocks.

The Granddaughter

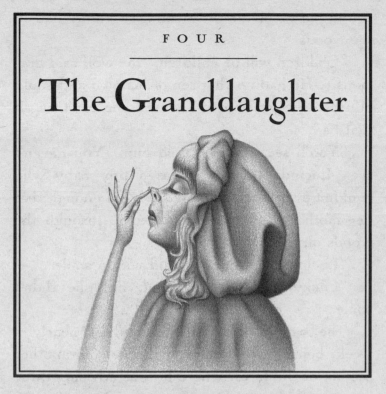

Once upon a time in a land and time when animals could speak and people could understand them, there lived an old woman whose best friend was a wolf. Because they were best friends, they told each other everything, and one of the things that Granny told the wolf was that she dreaded visits from her granddaughter, Lucinda.

"I'm afraid my son and his wife have spoiled her," Granny said to the wolf as they shared tea in the parlor of the little cottage Granny had in the woods.

"Children will be children," the wolf said graciously. He had no children of his own and could afford to be gracious. "I'm sure she can't be all that bad."

"You'll see," Granny told him. "You haven't seen Lucinda since she was a tiny baby who couldn't even talk, but now she's old enough that her mother has said she can come through the woods on her own to visit me."

"Lucky you," the wolf said with a smile.

"Lucky me," Granny said, but she didn't smile.

The wolf didn't visit Granny for nearly a week, being busy with wolf business in another section of the forest where he was advising three porcine brothers on home construction. After he came back, though, he was walking near the path leading from the meadow to Granny's house when he saw a little girl with a picnic basket. He recognized her right away from the picture Granny kept on her mantel.

"Hello," he said, loping up to the child. "You must be Lucinda."

"Don't call me that," the girl snapped. She

stopped to glare at him. "I'm Little Red Riding Hood."

The wolf paused to consider. "A little red riding hood is what you're wearing," he said. "It's not a name."

"It's my stage name," the girl said. She swirled her red cape dramatically. "I'm going to be a famous actress one day, and I'm going to travel all around the world, and when I do, all my clothes will be red velvet. It'll be my trademark."

The wolf nodded and opened his mouth, but before he could get a word out, Little Red continued: "Madame Yvette — she's my acting instructor — Madame Yvette says every great actor or actress needs a trademark. Mine will be red velvet because Madame Yvette says I look stunning in red velvet. Not everybody can carry off such a dramatic color, you know, but I have the coloring and the flair for it."

The wolf nodded and opened his mouth, but before he could get a sound out, Little Red continued: "I played Mary in our church's Easter pageant, and my performance was so touching everyone in the congregation wept — they actually wept. Even the priest had tears in his eyes, and you've got to believe he's seen an Easter pageant or two in his time, so you *know* I must have been stunning, even though they told me Mary had to wear white linen and not red velvet."

The wolf nodded, but before he could get his mouth open, Little Red continued: "When I go on tour, I'm going to demand that all the theaters I perform in must have red velvet seats, and I'll travel in a coach with red velvet cushions, and kings and queens and emperors and popes will stand in lines by the roads, waiting for hours for a chance to catch a glimpse of me."

Little Red paused for a breath.

The wolf was pretty sure there was only one pope, and that—since there was only the one— he probably wasn't permitted to stand on roadsides, waiting for actresses to pass by. But he didn't want to waste his opportunity to speak and decided he'd better say something important. He said: "Well, probably I should introduce myself—"

"Oh, I know who you are," Little Red interrupted. "You're that wolf who's my grandmother's friend. Yes, I noticed the scratch marks your claws left on her hardwood floors. I told her, I said, 'I don't know how you put up with it. I

mean, having a nonhuman friend is one thing,'
I told her, 'but scratches and dings on the floors
and furniture, which just make the whole house
look shabby, is another. After all, I have an image
to maintain for my fans.' "

Little Red leaned forward to lay her hand on
the wolf's shoulder. She didn't seem to notice that
his eyes were beginning to glaze over. She said,
"I know I can speak frankly with you because
you've been a friend of the family, so to speak,
for ages, so you've got to know I'm only telling
you this for your own good, but you really should
consider meeting my grandmother outside in the
garden. She could sit in a nice comfy lawn chair,
and then you wouldn't have to worry about
scratch marks or shedding or fleas or anything
like that."

Fleas? the wolf thought. *Fleas?*

But Little Red continued on. " 'And meanwhile,' I told Granny, 'have you ever tried Pro-
fessor Patterson's Wood-Replenishing Cream?
Madame Yvette uses it to polish the stage. It's
great for bringing out the natural shine of wood.'
Granny had never heard of it — which, of course,
I'd already guessed by the state her furniture was

in — but I told her I was sure my mother would be willing to spare a jar of hers, since Granny's floors were in such obviously desperate need."

Little Red stopped for another breath, but by then the wolf's head was spinning. He was just opening his mouth to protest that he did not have fleas, but he wasn't fast enough. Little Red started telling him about other products that her mother used around the home, and once she started, he wasn't able to get a word in edgewise.

After a few minutes that felt like an hour or two, the wolf was thinking that he was in serious danger of being bored to death.

The next time Little Red paused to inhale, he pointed at the sun overhead and exclaimed, all in one rush so Little Red couldn't interrupt, "My goodness, look at the time, I had no idea it was so late, I'm late for an appointment, it was real nice meeting you, good-bye!"

He also had the sense to start moving as soon as he started talking.

Which was a good thing, because Little Red started telling him, even as he left, about the clock her father had bought, which had been made in Switzerland, and it had a dial to show the phases of the moon and you could set it to any one of three different kinds of chimes, and it was carved with something-or-other — but by then the wolf had speeded up and was out of earshot.

He felt ready to collapse with exhaustion. The only thing that kept him going was the thought of poor Granny, and the knowledge that she had to be warned.

Luckily, he knew a shortcut.

Racing ahead, he got to Granny's house and pounded on the door.

Though it was midmorning, Granny came to the door wearing her nightie and slippers, with a shawl wrapped around her shoulders.

Before she could get a word out, the wolf said: "I met her, I know what you mean, she's on her way — quick, get dressed, there's still time to escape out the back door."

Granny sneezed. Twice. Three times. The wolf thought Little Red would probably blame him for giving her grandmother allergies, but Granny said, "She gave me her cold, and now I'm too sick to leave. I hoped her mother wouldn't let her come again today. What am I going to do? I'm not up to one of her visits."

"Tell her she can't come in," the wolf suggested.

"You can't say that to family," Granny said. She blew her nose in her hankie. "I can't face her. She'll tell me it isn't a cold and that I'm sneezing because of all the dust in my house. Can you believe she told me my house is one huge dust trap and that her mother wouldn't stand for it?"

"Yes," the wolf said, "I believe it." Looking out the window, he added, "Here she comes up the walk."

"She's sure to have all sorts of remedies and advice," Granny said. "Well, I'm hiding in the closet. Call me when it's safe to come out again."

She stepped into the closet and pulled the door closed behind her.

Something has to be done about that little girl, the wolf thought, *or she'll never leave.* He grabbed a spare nightie and nightcap out of the chest at the foot of the bed and leapt into Granny's bed, pulling the covers up to his chin just as Little Red walked in without knocking or waiting for an invitation.

"I got the most beautiful azaleas out of our garden for you to cheer you up," Little Red said, reaching into her basket, "along with the regular cakes and bread and jams and other goodies my mother usually packs for you. I'll bet you thought it was too early in the year for azaleas, but we have the very first ones, because what we do is we force them by putting burlap bags on the ground to . . ."

Little Red stopped talking, and it was the first time the wolf had heard such a thing.

"What are you doing here?" she demanded.

"Why, dear," the wolf said, trying to sound like Granny, "I'm your grandmother. I live here."

"You're not Granny," Little Red said. "You're that rude wolf."

Rude! the wolf thought. "No, dear," he insisted in a high, shaky voice, "I'm Granny. I'm feeling much better today, but very contagious. Why don't you leave the basket of goodies on the night table and go back home?"

Little Red put the basket down on the floor, but she picked up a wooden spoon with which Granny had been eating a bowl of oatmeal, and she approached the bed. "If you're Granny," she said, and jabbed the wolf's front leg with the spoon, "why do you have such big, hairy arms?"

The wolf winced but ignored the oatmeal, which stuck to his fur. He forced himself to speak gently and lovingly. "The better to hug you with, my dear," he said.

"And if you're Granny, why do you have such big, hairy ears?" She poked him on the side of the head with the spoon, leaving behind another glob of oatmeal.

"Ouch! The better to hear you with, my dear." He forced himself to smile.

"And if you're Granny, why do you have such big, sharp teeth?" She smacked him on the muzzle with the spoon — which hurt a lot.

The wolf lost his temper. "The better to eat you with!" he yelled. He didn't mean it, of course. He was angry, but not angry enough to eat his best friend's granddaughter.

But as he jumped out of bed, intending only to frighten Little Red a bit, his back leg caught on the blankets and he half fell on her.

Landing heavily on the floor, she began to scream.

Loudly.

Very loudly.

Extemely loudly.

She scrambled backward, knocking Granny's chair over, and continued screaming, all the while whacking away at the wolf with the wooden spoon.

The wolf, still caught in the bed linens, flailed

about, shredding the sheets with his claws, and began to howl.

Granny, hearing all the commotion, tried to open the closet door, but the tipped chair was in the way. She was sure an intruder had come into the house and was killing both her best friend and her granddaughter. "Help!" she began to scream, knowing that there were woodcutters working nearby. "Help!"

And one of the woodcutters, a neighbor man named Bob, heard her.

Bob shifted his ax to his left hand and swept up his hunting musket as he took off running across Granny's yard.

Throwing open the front door, he saw the snarling wolf dressed in Granny's clothes, and he saw Little Red, still on the floor, screaming. He assumed the worst and fired the musket . . .

. . . just as he stepped into Little Red's basket of goodies.

The bullet missed the wolf and shattered the bowl of oatmeal on the night table.

"What idiot's shooting guns off in my house?" Granny yelled, but nobody could hear her because of Little Red's screaming.

Bob dropped the musket, which was only

good for one shot before it needed to be reloaded, and switched the ax back to his right hand, all the while trying to shake the basket off his foot at the same time he was approaching the bed. Dragging Little Red out of the way, he swung his ax at the wolf . . .

. . . just as Granny heaved herself against the closet door, scraping the fallen chair across the floor.

The ax embedded itself in the edge of the door.

Granny looked from the ax head, three inches away from her nose, to Bob.

There was a moment of stunned silence. The wolf stopped struggling against the tangled bedsheets. Even Little Red stopped screaming.

"What in the world did you do that for?" Granny demanded.

"I thought the wolf ate you," Bob said. "I was trying to rescue your granddaughter."

Too shocked for words, the wolf shook his head to indicate he'd never eat Granny.

"Well!" Little Red said. "Some rescue! First you barge in here, tracking your muddy boots all over the floor" — Bob opened his mouth to apologize, but Little Red continued — "which I know wasn't in very good shape to begin with, Granny being the indifferent housekeeper she is — I know she doesn't mind my saying that because I only mention it for her own good, and believe me, when I'm a famous actress I'll hire a maid to give her a hand, because, heaven knows, she isn't getting any younger." The wolf saw that Bob's eyes were beginning to bulge as his hand slipped from the handle of his ax, but Little Red continued: "But even leaving Granny's messy habits out of it, you come in here trailing big globs of mud and grass, shoot a hole through the bowl, which *my family* bought Granny for Christmas last year, gouge a perfectly fine door with your ax, not to mention pulling my hair, and look at this — *look at this!*" Everybody looked. "You are stepping in the goodies my mother made and which I brought here for my sick granny, never mind that I had to walk for hours to get here and that I'm even now missing a class with Madame Yvette to be here, inhaling wolf dander and catching a chill from sitting on this floor, which no doubt will ruin my stunning speaking voice. And you call this a rescue?"

Bob shook the basket off his foot.

The wolf saw that the azaleas were crunched,

but the food was surprisingly undamaged. He straightened the nightcap, which had fallen to cover one eye. He, Granny, and Bob looked at one another. They looked at the basket of goodies. They looked at Little Red.

There was only one thing they could do.

They locked Little Red in the closet, then they went out in the backyard and had a picnic.

FIVE

Excuses

Where did the children of Hamlin go,
following the piper's song,
across the patterned fields
and through the woods
and into a crack in the mountain
that wasn't there before
and will never be there again?

If he truly meant them ill,
he might have drowned them with the rats.
But if he truly meant them well,
he might have forgiven their families.

And did he have a family of his own,
demanding explanations for
a townful of children trailing along behind?
And what does a magical piper say
in such a case:
"Look what followed me home —
can I keep them?"

SIX

Jack

Once upon a time, after the invention of teenagers but before there were shopping malls for teenagers to hang around in, there lived a young man named Jack.

Jack was a lazy boy. When his mother asked him to help around the house, he always said, "I'm too tired," and when his mother asked him when he was going to get a job, he always said, "Tomorrow." Until, one day, Jack's mother told

him that — unless he started looking for a job —
the next time he left the house to visit his friends,
she was going to change the locks on the doors
so he couldn't get back in.

Jack decided this would be a good time to go
to the village to see what sorts of jobs there were.
But being the lazy boy he was, he didn't want to
walk. And being the lazy boy he was, he hadn't
earned any money to buy a horse. So Jack rode
his mother's cow into the village.

"That's a fine cow," the tavern keeper said
when he saw Jack ride up the street. "I was just
telling my wife that we should get a cow of our
own since we have so many children."

"A cow is a very nice thing to have," said
Jack. This looking-for-a-job was not as hard as
he had thought it would be, he decided. He could
get a job in the cow-selling business. "How much
would you give me for this cow?" he asked.

"Ah, well," said the tavern keeper. "Times are
tight. I don't have any spare cash. But I could
give you a free meal and all the beer you can
drink. There's a party going on in the tavern right
now. Feel free to join in."

So Jack handed the tavern keeper the rope
that was tied to the cow's halter. As far as Jack

was concerned, he didn't have much choice: What other job was he likely to find besides cow salesman? And where else was he going to find someone who wanted to buy a cow?

In the tavern, the tavern keeper's wife thanked Jack for the cow and brought him a bowl of bean soup and a mug of beer. Beer after beer Jack drank. The people in the tavern talked and laughed and sang, and the afternoon became evening, and the evening became night, and the night became earliest morning.

"It's time for the tavern to close," the tavern keeper said to Jack, who was spread facedown on the bean-soup-and-beer-splattered table.

Jack just snored.

"Everybody else has gone home," the tavern keeper's wife said. "It's time for you to go home, too."

Jack just snored.

They tipped Jack off the table, but still he did not wake up.

The tavern keeper's oldest son, who was not a lazy boy, rolled Jack out into the street and closed the door behind him.

At the sound of the *thump* so close to his head, Jack woke up. All the other shops in the village had closed hours earlier, so there were no lights flickering in windows. Jack was lying flat on his back in a totally dark street, looking up at the stars.

"Oh," he said, because he was very, very drunk from all that beer, "I must be in the sky. I must be in a city in the sky."

As exciting as this thought was, Jack went back to sleep.

Now at about this same time, Effie, the potter's daughter, was coming home from a church dance. Her father had told her she could stay till midnight, and here it was just about dawn, so she was hurrying along the street trying to think of good excuses. When you're six hours late and you've already been warned once and you don't have *any* excuse — much less a good one — it's hard to think of much else.

Effie wasn't watching where she was going and she tripped over Jack.

Which woke Jack up yet again.

"Oh my," Effie said. "Are you all right? I hope you're all right. You are, aren't you?" She took a few more steps, but Jack didn't get up. Since Effie would never lie down in the middle of the street — dark hours of the morning or not —

she assumed there was something wrong with Jack; and since she had just tripped over him, she was afraid she was the cause of whatever was wrong with him. She walked back and leaned over him. "Please say you're all right," she said. "I really *have* to be getting home or my father will kill me."

Jack focused his eyes on Effie leaning over him. "Whoa!" he said. "You're a tall one, aren't you?"

Effie, who wasn't tall but *was* in a rush said, "Yes. Fine. Whatever you say. Are you all right?"

Jack said, "Are all the people who live in the city in the sky so tall?"

Which didn't sound at all to Effie as though he were all right. "Oh dear," she said, "what am I going to do with you?"

"Good night," Jack said, and went back to sleep yet again.

Well, Effie told herself, if he was going to be like that, there really wasn't much she could do.

Home was just a few houses away, and once again she started walking.

But then she stopped again.

It really isn't any of my business, she told herself. She took another step.

It's not like I even know him, she told herself. She took yet another step.

It makes no difference to me if the next person to come by trips over him, she told herself. And she took three more steps, one after the other.

But the next person to come by might be in a horse-drawn cart, which would prove disastrous for anyone lying in the street talking about cities in the sky.

What are you going to do? Effie asked herself. *He's obviously in no condition to walk, and you certainly can't carry him.*

By this time Effie had reached the gate to her yard. She couldn't see any candlelight leaking out from around the shutters, which probably meant that her father had gone to bed rather than waiting up for her. Good news for her, bad news for Jack.

Maybe she could find a rope, Effie thought. She could tie it to Jack's legs and drag him out of harm's way. Not that bouncing his head along the cobblestones was likely to improve his thinking.

But then, even better than a rope, Effie spotted her father's wheelbarrow in the garden. She had been weeding before stopping to get ready for the dance, and now here it was: still half full of weeds, but at least not locked up in the shed.

Effie tipped the wheelbarrow up on its one big wheel and pushed it, jostling and bumping against the cobblestones, back to where Jack lay. She nudged Jack with her foot. "Get up," she said. "I've come to rescue you from early-morning milk deliveries and from Wilbur Stillmanson bringing his pigs to market."

Jack opened his eyes and looked all that distance up to Effie's face. "Oh," he said. "It's the lady giant again."

"Yes," Effie said, to get him moving. "Come on. Get up. Get in here."

Shakily, Jack managed to get to his feet.

For about two seconds.

He stumbled and fell facedown into the wheelbarrow, which wobbled but did not tip over.

With Jack's legs hanging over the edge, Effie started pushing the wheelbarrow back to her house.

Jack's nose was being tickled by the mattress of vines and leaves he was lying on. He didn't like to complain about the bumpy ride, since the lady giant was helping him, but he asked, "Do I need rescuing?"

"Yes," Effie said. "Keep your voice down. If you wake up my father, we'll both need rescuing."

Ah, Jack told himself. *The lady giant's father is an ogre.* He passed out again.

Effie considered leaving Jack in the wheelbarrow out in the garden. But it was already getting light out, and if her father came outside, he'd be sure to see him. Which would leave her with a lot of questions to answer. So she decided it would be better to wheel Jack around to the workshop door and bring him into the house the back way.

After pushing him all the way up the hill and over the door jamb, when she realized Jack was asleep again, she tipped him out onto the floor.

"Ow," Jack said, shaking twigs and leaves out of his hair. "Where are we, lady giant?"

"*Shh,*" Effie warned.

But it was too late.

"Effie?" her father's voice called from his bedroom, down the hall. "Effie, is that you?"

Effie motioned for Jack to keep still. "Yes, Father," she answered in her sweetest, most innocent voice.

Which, of course, made her father suspicious.

"Are you just now getting back home?" he asked.

"No, I've been home for hours," Effie answered. "I've been to bed and now I'm up getting breakfast."

But she could hear the door to her father's room open and she realized he was coming to check.

"If he finds us here together, he's going to kill both of us!" she whispered frantically to Jack. But where could she hide him? She had a suspicion Jack couldn't make it the five whole steps to the door. She cast a hurried look around her father's workshop. Under the table that held the potter's wheel? Too open. Behind the drying racks? Only if Jack could stand still and not tip over. She couldn't count on that. Effie touched the side of the kiln to see if it was hot. It wasn't. "Quick!" she whispered to Jack. "Get in the oven. Father won't be using it today."

Jack, who thought he was in a kitchen, staggered back, overwhelmed by the size of the kiln. "That's one big oven, lady giant," he said.

"Yes," Effie said. This "lady giant" business was becoming annoying. She shoved him in and slammed the door.

But she didn't latch it, so that he could breathe. From the crack along the edge, Jack watched as Effie's father walked into the room.

"Are you just getting back?" her father asked again.

"No," Effie said, hastily tying on an apron to cover her party dress. "I came in here for wood to get the kitchen fire going for breakfast."

Her father sniffed the air. "What's that I smell?" he asked. But he knew what he smelled — he smelled beer; he just wanted to know where the smell was coming from. "Is that you?" he demanded.

"No, Father," Effie said.

He sniffed her, but the beer smell didn't seem to be coming from her. "It better not be you," he warned.

Meanwhile Jack, in the oven, thought, *Oh, no! He can smell me! He must be a man-eating giant.* Jack began to work out his last will and testament.

Effie picked up two pieces of split log and left, bringing them into the kitchen to start the breakfast fire.

Her father stayed in the workshop, rechecking the glaze on the cups and bowls and jugs that had come out of the kiln the day before.

Jack realized that he didn't own anything worth leaving to anybody.

There was a loud crash from the kitchen. Jack heard Effie cry out, then there was the sound of glass breaking and the frantic squawking of a chicken. "You get back here," Effie shouted.

"Effie?" her father called.

Jack saw Effie come back into the workshop, holding by the legs a flapping, squawking, feather-shedding hen. "She did it again," Effie said, shaking the hen. "The miserable little beast. I took off my gold bracelet before I started working and this . . . this . . . THING . . . ate it."

Her father pried open the hen's beak. "I can't see it, Effie," he said. He took the hen from his daughter and plunked her down on the table. "Lay," he commanded.

The hen protested some more.

"*Lay!*" he shouted.

And then, to Jack's amazement, the hen laid a golden egg.

"You wretched thing," Effie told the hen. "I liked my bracelet better." And to her father she said, "We should have *her* for breakfast and be done with."

"Now, now," her father said. "She was a gift

from my brother." He let go of the hen, who ruffled her feathers and half flew, half ran to the shelf along the back of the table.

Leaning forward to see through the crack where the door didn't meet the oven, Jack saw the hen brush against a cloth-draped object that stood about as tall as Jack's arm was long. From this mysterious-looking object there came a sound somewhere between human voice and musical notes, as though the hen had jostled . . . what? Something magical, Jack was sure.

Just while Jack was wondering why someone would keep a magical musical anything bundled up in the kitchen, Effie said, "And that singing harp! A gift from your sister. We need to get a better class of relatives."

A gold-egg-laying hen! Jack thought. *A singing harp!* He thought of how, minutes ago, he had come to the realization that he didn't own anything worthwhile. Wouldn't his mother stop complaining that he didn't have a job if he owned a gold-egg-laying hen? Wouldn't his friends be impressed by a singing harp?

"Now, now, Effie," Effie's father said again. "We can't just throw them away. Come Christmas

I'll wrap them up in pretty paper and give them away as door prizes at the Potters' Guild Christmas party."

"That's four months away," Effie protested.

"So long as we keep the harp covered," her father said, "and we're careful not to leave gold lying around —"

But Effie wasn't finished. "And what about that magic cauldron-of-plenty your aunt gave us that never runs out of food," she demanded, "except the only food it has is pickled liver? I'm always tripping over that thing."

"Well, you don't need to keep it in the kitchen," her father said. "Here, I'll help you move it. . . ."

Jack watched as the two of them moved out of the room, then he turned his attention to the wonderful hen. It was settling down on the shelf, looking ready — in Jack's estimation — to lay another egg. It wasn't fair, he thought, for the giants to have so much good fortune when he had none. He leaned against the oven door for a better look, and the door swung open and Jack fell out.

The hen began to cluck nervously.

"*Shh,*" Jack said.

But this only made the hen think he was a snake, and she squawked even louder.

Jack came closer, still going *"Shh,"* intending nothing more than to try to hush the hen, but now the singing harp became nervous, too. From beneath its cloth draping it asked in a silvery, musical voice, "What's happening?"

"Shh," Jack said again. "I'm not supposed to be here. You'll get me in trouble."

And then the harp, being a clever harp, knew what that meant. *"THIEF!"* the harp cried. *"THIEF! THIEF! THIEF!"*

From down the hall Effie's father echoed, "Thief?" and Jack thought, *Well. Why not?* So he grabbed the hen with one hand and the singing harp, cover and all, with the other and jumped out the window, landing in the garden.

Jack took one step, tripped over an ivy vine, and went sprawling. He tucked the hen and the harp in close to him under his jacket so they wouldn't get injured and rolled down, down the hill until he came to rest with his face pressed against the bars of the gate by the street.

He got to his feet, dizzy and bruised but still holding on to both hen and harp. He looked over his shoulder and there was Effie's father running toward him, holding a huge black cooking pot and calling, "The cauldron, the cauldron, too!"

Sure that if he wasn't fast enough he was going to get eaten, Jack squeezed through the bars of the gate and took off down the street.

After a while he couldn't hear the sound of pursuing footsteps anymore, and when he looked over his shoulder there was no sign that he was being followed. But just in case, he never slowed down. He ran and ran, all the way home, bursting through the kitchen door just as his mother was sitting down to breakfast.

"Jack!" she said, seeing him covered with twigs and dirt. "What's happened?"

Jack flung himself into a chair, panting loudly.

"I thought you went to town to look for a job," his mother said.

"I did," Jack gasped between wheezing breaths. "And I found one, too. I'm a cow salesman."

"*Cow salesman!*" his mother cried. "What kind of job is that when we only have one cow?"

"Oh," Jack said. "Good point."

His mother rested her head in her hands. "I hope you at least got a good price for her."

"Ahm . . ." Jack said, reaching into his pocket. He came out with a handful of lumpy, beer-encrusted beans.

"That's disgusting." His mother pulled on his sleeve until his arm was hanging out the window and shook the mess off his hand. "You were gone a whole day and night, and all you come home with is a handful of beans?" she shouted.

Jack wished his mother wouldn't be so loud; his head felt as though it was about to burst like a dropped egg. Which reminded him . . . He reached under his jacket and pulled out the hen, which he set on the table.

His mother looked at him skeptically. "You traded our cow for a chicken?" she demanded.

Jack shook his head, which he shouldn't have done, not with his headache, then he said, "No. The beans must have been magical beans. They grew into this incredible . . . well, I guess it must have been a beanstalk . . . which reached up, up, up . . . to a city in the sky."

"A city in the sky," his mother repeated.

"Giants lived there," Jack continued. "The lady giant tried to help me. She hid me in the oven. But the man giant could smell people. He was going to eat me."

"*She* put you in the oven," Jack's mother said, "But *he* was the one you were afraid of?"

"And they had this hen that lays golden eggs and this harp"—Jack pulled the cloth-draped harp out from under his jacket—"that sings. I barely escaped with my life. The giant was chasing after me with a cooking pot."

"You *stole* these things?" Jack's mother cried in horror. "Did I raise my son to *steal* things?"

"They didn't want them," Jack protested.

"A hen that lays golden eggs and a harp that sings—*and they didn't want them?*"

Jack squirmed. But before he could think of how to answer, the hen clucked loudly, sat down, and laid an egg. A perfectly white, perfectly ordinary egg.

Jack's mother just looked at Jack.

Jack sighed. "I guess I forgot to mention that you have to feed the hen gold before she lays golden eggs."

"But we don't have any gold," his mother pointed out.

"But we will." Jack pulled the cover off the harp. "People will come from miles around to hear this. They'll pay us. Sing, harp," he commanded.

And the harp did.

In loud, off-key, gooey, sticky, ear-shattering, eye-watering, fingernails-on-blackboard notes.

Jack's mother put her head down on the table and covered her ears. "Stop," she cried. "Make it stop."

Jack threw the cover back over the harp.

Eventually the harp stopped singing.

"Oops," Jack said.

Jack's mother raised her head, then looked frantically at the door. "Jack!" she said. "What was that noise? Is that the giant outside?"

Jack leapt to his feet, listening, though he hadn't heard anything.

His mother said, "You better take the ax and check."

Jack got the ax from beside the door.

"Look in the barn and all around the yard," his mother advised.

"All right," Jack said.

While he was gone, his mother changed the locks.

And Now a Word from Our Sponsor

Rapunzel, Rapunzel,
let down your hair.
See it shine; see it bounce.
No split ends.
Strong enough to climb up:
For the right price,
you, too, can have hair like this.

The Bridge

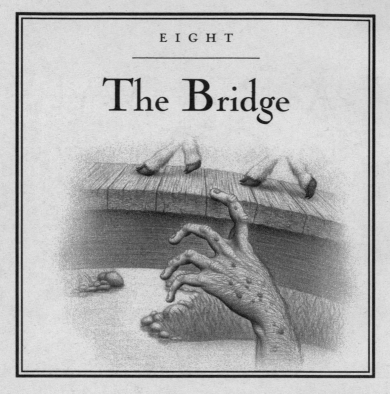

Once upon a time before there were toll bridges, there were troll bridges.

One day three billy goat brothers were munching on the tall, sweet grass on the south side of a river, when the smallest and youngest of the billy goats happened to look up and notice that the grass on the north side of the river was taller yet and looked even sweeter. So the smallest billy goat headed off across the bridge, his tiny hooves going *click-click* over the wooden boards.

When he got halfway across, however, a long, skinny, hairy hand reached out from underneath the bridge and grabbed hold of his leg.

"Mmmm," a troll voice said, and the smallest billy goat could hear the smacking of troll lips. "This looks like a tasty treat for a midmorning snack."

"Oh, please don't eat me," the smallest billy goat pleaded. "I'm so small and skinny, it would hardly be worth the effort of eating me."

"A mouthful is better than none," the troll said, dragging the smallest billy goat closer and closer to the edge of the bridge.

"Yes, but," the smallest billy goat said, catching a glimpse of yellow troll eyes and sharp troll teeth, "my older brother, who's much bigger than I am, is right behind me. If you eat me, he's sure to see, and he'll never come across. If you let me go, you can eat him."

The troll looked over the smallest billy goat's shoulder and saw that there was, indeed, a somewhat larger billy goat approaching. The troll licked the smallest billy goat's leg but then let him go.

The smallest billy goat trotted across the

bridge as fast as his skinny legs would carry him.

The middle billy goat — who was middle both in size and age — had noticed the tall, sweet-looking grass on the north side of the river, and now he saw his brother was there. So the middle billy goat headed off across the bridge, his medium-size hooves going *tap-tap* over the wooden boards.

When he got halfway across, however, a long, skinny, hairy hand reached out from underneath the bridge and grabbed hold of his leg.

"Mmmm," a troll voice said, and the middle billy goat could hear the smacking of troll lips. "This looks like a tasty treat for lunch."

"Oh, please don't eat me," the middle billy goat pleaded. "I'm so small and skinny, it would hardly be worth the effort of eating me."

"Two mouthfuls is better than none," the troll said, dragging the middle billy goat closer and closer to the edge of the bridge.

"Yes, but," the middle billy goat said, catching a glimpse of yellow troll eyes and sharp troll teeth, "my oldest brother, who's much, much bigger than I am, is right behind me. If you eat me, he's sure to see and he'll never come across. If you let me go, you can eat him."

The troll looked over the middle billy goat's shoulder and saw that there was, indeed, a quite large billy goat approaching. The troll licked the middle billy goat's leg but then let him go.

The middle billy goat trotted across the bridge as fast as his medium-size legs would carry him.

The biggest and oldest of the billy goats had seen how the grass across the river looked tall and sweet. He now saw one brother was there and the other about to join him. So the largest billy goat headed off across the bridge, his big hooves going *thump-thump* over the wooden boards.

When he got halfway across, however, a long, skinny, hairy hand reached out from underneath the bridge and grabbed hold of his leg.

"Mmmm," a troll voice said, and the biggest billy goat could hear the smacking of troll lips. "This looks like a tasty treat for dinner."

"I'm not dinner," the biggest billy goat said, "I'm a billy goat."

"You're dinner now," the troll said, dragging the biggest billy goat closer and closer to the edge of the bridge.

But just when the troll got the biggest billy goat where it thought it wanted him, the biggest billy goat lowered his large head and with a powerful jab of his huge horns, he knocked the troll off the bridge and into the water.

Then the biggest billy goat went *thump-thump* the rest of the way across the bridge.

"Good work," the smallest billy goat said.

"Good work," the middle billy goat said.

"Thanks for the warning," the biggest billy goat said. "I could have gotten killed."

And with that he knocked both of them into the water and ate all the tall, sweet grass himself.

NINE

Rated PG-13

Fairy-tale endings you're not likely to see:

—after growing into a beautiful swan, the Ugly Duckling pecks all his tormentors to death.

—the Emperor orders the execution of everyone who's seen him naked.

—the lazy cat, dog, and mouse suffocate the Little Red Hen with her own cake.

—the elves lock the Shoemaker and his wife in

the basement, take all their money, and run off to Central America, where they operate a pirate radio station.

— the Gingerbread Man turns out to be carnivorous and eats the fox.

— Snow White and Sleeping Beauty simply refuse to get out of bed.

— when a portion of the sky really does fall, Chicken Little becomes the leader of her own religious movement; she gets her own TV show, collects millions of dollars to build a theme park, then makes off with the money, joining the elves in Central America.

TEN

Mattresses

Once upon a time, before the invention of water-beds or air mattresses or Craftmatic adjustable beds, there lived a prince named Royal. Because Prince Royal had such a royal name, great things were expected of him, and when it was time for him to marry, everyone agreed that he needed to find absolutely the most perfect princess to be his wife.

One rainy night while the search for the most

perfect princess was still going on, there came a knocking at the door of the castle. The servants opened the door and there stood a most lovely girl, wearing satins and silks and furs, just like a princess, but she was totally drenched, as though she'd been swimming in her fine clothes.

"I am Princess Courtney of Winthrop," she said when she was led into the presence of Prince Royal and his mother, the queen, in the audience chamber. "I've accidentally gotten separated from my traveling companions, and now I'm lost and wet and cold and hungry. May I please spend the night in your castle?"

Prince Royal fell in love immediately. He just stood there, with his hand over his racing heart, unable to remember how to speak. The queen, seeing this, answered graciously, "Of course, my dear," and ordered the servants to prepare a room for Princess Courtney, to find her dry clothes, and to prepare a meal for her.

"Oh my," Prince Royal said as soon as Princess Courtney was escorted from the audience chamber. "Isn't she the most perfect princess you've ever seen?"

"Well," the queen agreed, "she's certainly very beautiful."

Later, at dinner, as the princess ate daintily, always knowing which of the several forks and spoons to use, Prince Royal leaned over to his mother and asked, "Isn't she the most perfect princess you've ever seen?"

"Well," the queen agreed, "she certainly has elegant manners."

After that, when Prince Royal had finally remembered how to speak, he and Princess Courtney spoke of politics and philosophy and art.

That night, when Prince Royal stopped by his mother's room to wish her a good night, he sighed and said, "Isn't she the most perfect princess you've ever seen?"

"Well," the queen agreed, "she certainly is very intelligent and eloquent."

Prince Royal went to bed, planning that in the morning he would ask Princess Courtney to marry him, since she was obviously the most perfect princess in the world. But no sooner had he set his head to his pillow than he heard a loud scream from the princess's bedroom.

The prince, the queen, and all the servants ran to the princess's door. "Courtney, angel," Prince Royal called, "what's the matter?"

Princess Courtney threw open the door and

stood leaning weakly against the door frame, one hand pressed to her back.

"What happened?" Prince Royal asked, putting his arm around her because she was obviously shaken.

Princess Courtney pointed to the bed. "That, that . . . *thing!*"

"The bed, my dear?" asked the queen, as though perhaps Princess Courtney had forgotten the word.

"That torture device," Princess Courtney said. "What's the mattress stuffed with?"

The queen went to the bed and pressed against the mattress. "Why, it's stuffed with the down of baby swans, the way all our mattresses are. Do you have allergies?"

"Of course not," the princess snapped. "But your baby swans feel as if they must have rocks and shards of glass instead of down. Don't you feel the lumps and bumps and sharp things?"

The queen felt and felt but could find nothing.

Prince Royal hugged Princess Courtney and said, "The most perfect princesses are very delicate."

"Yes," the queen said. "Well, someone go fetch another mattress."

Another mattress was brought and was set upon the first.

"I'm sure that will be much better," Princess Courtney said.

Prince Royal kissed her hand good night and everybody trooped out of the room.

But Prince Royal had no sooner closed the door to his room than he heard a horrible shriek from Princess Courtney's room.

Everybody met once again in front of her door, calling out, "What is it? What's happened?"

Princess Courtney flung open the door, moaning and holding on to her back with both hands this time. "Oh, the anguish, the torment!" she murmured.

Again the queen felt the bed; again she found nothing wrong. "Bring up two more mattresses," she ordered. "And a step stool so the princess can get up." She patted the princess's shoulder. "There, there," she said. "Four mattresses will make it better."

Princess Courtney smiled graciously.

But once the two additional mattresses were brought and set in place — and once the queen, the prince, and all the servants had stepped out into the hall—the night was once again pierced by Princess Courtney's frantic cries for help.

She came to the door, staggering, her hair wild, her clothes disheveled.

Prince Royal patted her hand while the servants went to fetch the five additional mattresses and the stepladder the queen had ordered. "That makes nine mattresses in all," Prince Royal told the princess. "Surely that will be enough."

"If not," Princess Courtney said, "I will try to bear my pain bravely."

As Prince Royal and the queen left the room, Prince Royal whispered to his mother, "She's brave, too. Isn't she the most perfect princess you've ever seen?"

"Well," the queen said, "she certainly is very delicate, even for a princess."

This time Prince Royal not only made it back into his room but even into his bed. He lay his head on his pillow and thought of his brave princess. He yawned. He closed his eyes. He became aware of a sound, not a scream or a shriek or a cry, but a soft whimpering.

Prince Royal got up and knocked on Princess Courtney's door. "Courtney, angel, is everything all right?" He could hear her sobbing.

"Oh, the pain, the pain."

"Courtney, angel, open the door and we'll get you more mattresses."

"I can't," the princess cried. "I've been crippled by the pain."

So Prince Royal had to call for the kingdom's battering ram and twelve strong men-at-arms, who knocked down the door. Prince Royal climbed up the stepladder and lifted the princess off the nine mattresses.

"I tried so hard to be brave," she whispered, "but it was more than my body could endure."

The queen, who had been awakened by the door coming down, ordered ten more mattresses and a full-size ladder.

This time everyone stayed in the room until Princess Courtney was perched on top of her pile of nineteen mattresses. "How is that, my dear?" the queen asked.

Princess Courtney winced but said quietly, "It will do."

In the hallway, Prince Royal turned to his mother.

His mother said, in a tone she'd never used with him before: "Go to bed, Royal."

There were no more major disturbances in the

night, but all night long they could hear—since the door was gone—the bed springs creaking and the princess sighing.

The next morning, Princess Courtney came to breakfast all stooped over and with bags under her eyes, though she still looked lovely. Actually the queen had bags under her eyes, too, and so did Prince Royal and the servants who were setting out the breakfast.

The queen asked, "Didn't you sleep well, my dear, once there were nineteen mattresses?"

"I tossed and turned all night," Princess Courtney said. "It was as though all those mattress were perched upon a pointy mountain."

While arrangements were being made for the princess to be returned to her own castle, Prince Royal and the queen went back up to her room. The queen climbed the ladder and lay on the mattresses.

"Do you feel the pointy mountain?" Prince Royal asked.

"No," his mother said. "But then I'm a queen, not a princess."

Still, she ordered the servants to take away all nineteen mattresses so she could examine the bed frame.

"Ah!" she said.

"Ah?" Prince Royal asked.

The queen picked up a single squashed pea, which had somehow made its way under the first mattress. "This was what she felt."

Prince Royal leaned closer to see. "It's quite small," he said.

"Yes, it is," his mother agreed.

"I guess this shows that Courtney is, indeed, a perfect princess, that she could feel such a tiny thing under all those mattresses."

"It does show that," the queen admitted.

"But it also shows she's very fussy," Prince Royal said.

"Hard to get along with," the queen added.

"Impossible to please," Prince Royal finished.

So they waved good-bye when Princess Courtney set out for home, and Prince Royal never did ask her to marry him.

And after she was gone, everybody went back to bed.

ELEVEN

Twins

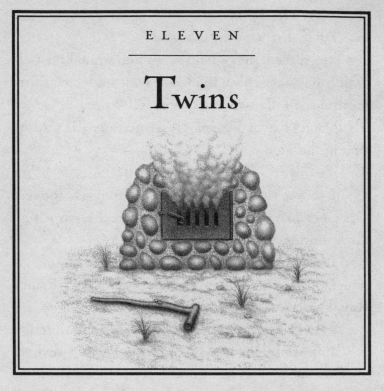

Once upon a time, before Medicare or golden-age retirement communities, there lived a beautiful young girl named Isabella, who stayed at home to take care of her parents. The boys in the village would whistle when they walked by her house and they'd call out, "Isabella, come out and play," or "Isabella, come see Clarence's new puppy," or "Isabella, will you watch us race?"

But Isabella always said no, she had to take care of her parents.

The years passed, and Isabella became a beautiful young woman. The young men of the village would carry flowers to her door and they'd say, "Isabella, come out for a picnic," or "Isabella, come to the dance," or "Isabella, will you kiss me?"

But Isabella always said no, she had to take care of her parents.

Until the day Isabella's parents died.

All the young men she had grown up with had married long ago, or they had left the village to seek their fortunes. There were new young men, of course. But — although they knew Isabella as a kind and gentle woman — they were too young to remember when Isabella had been young and beautiful, and they never came knocking at her door.

Then one day, one of her old suitors who had left the village came back. He was stooped and haggard, looking older than he was, and more wary and suspicious than Isabella remembered. The man's name was Siegfried and he was a woodcutter who lived in a small cottage in the forest. But his wife had just died and he needed help to raise his two small children.

Isabella was horrified when she learned that Siegfried had left his children alone in the cottage in the woods while he came to the village, and she immediately agreed to marry him and take care of all of them.

And beautiful children they were, Isabella thought when she and her new husband arrived back at the cottage, as beautiful as the carved marble angels over the doors of the cathedral. A boy and a girl, obviously twins, they couldn't have been older than six or seven.

"Hansel," Siegfried said to the boy, "Gretel," he said to the girl, "say hello to your new mother."

Isabella stooped down to hug the children, but Gretel said, "She's not our mother."

And Hansel said, "Our mother's dead." Then he added, "Our mother didn't love us."

And Gretel finished, "She wouldn't have died if she did."

How incredibly sad, Isabella thought. *Oh, the poor, sweet dears.* Her eyes filled with tears for the sad, sad children. "Of course your mother loved you," she said. "She didn't *want* to leave you. And I'm not here to replace her. Nobody could ever do that. But I'm here to love you and take care of you just the way your mother did."

"How can you love us . . ." Hansel started.

And Gretel finished, ". . . when you've only just met us?"

The two children looked at each other. Their expressions never changed. In fact, Isabella thought, they really *had* no expressions: not happy, nor sad, nor angry. Just . . . *there.*

She said, "But your father's told me so much about you."

Which wasn't true. All he had said was that their mother had died and that he needed help to raise them. He hadn't even said how their mother had died.

Now the children were looking at each other again, in silence. Simultaneously their gaze went back to Isabella. *They know I just lied,* she guessed. It had seemed such a kind and harmless thing to say.

"Children," Siegfried murmured as though begging them to give Isabella a chance.

Still without a word, the children turned to leave.

"Wait," Isabella called. "I have brought you gifts."

The children stopped. Turned. Waited.

Isabella went to the small bag in which she had packed all her worldly possessions. "Hansel," she called, but both children approached. "Hold out your hand."

Hansel did.

Gretel watched with large, pale, unblinking eyes.

Isabella put her father's gold pocket watch into his palm, letting the chain run through her fingers one last time. "This was my father's," she said. "His father was a famous watchmaker, and he made it."

Hansel watched her with large, pale, unblinking eyes.

"Hold it up to your ear," Isabella said, trying to get him to bend his elbow. "Listen to it tick."

Gretel said, "We're too little to know how to tell time."

"But you can learn." Isabella felt her heart sinking.

Hansel said, "There's never anyplace to go in the woods. And no special time to be there." He moved to hand the watch back to Isabella, but she wouldn't take it.

"Keep it," she told him. "You may want it

when you're older." To Gretel she said, "I have something for you, too. From my mother." But now her hand shook. Isabella took Gretel's cold hand and placed her mother's wedding ring on one of the child's fingers.

"It's too big," Hansel said as his sister lifted her hand and pointed her tiny fingers down, letting the ring fall back into Isabella's hand.

"You'll grow into it," Isabella said, putting the ring back on Gretel's finger.

"It isn't something to wear in the woods," Gretel said. Again she let the ring drop from her finger.

And Hansel let the watch drop.

Isabella stopped the ring from rolling under the bed, but the glass on the watch had cracked. "I'm sorry," she said, "there was no time to buy or make . . ." But when she looked up, the children had left and she could see them walking hand in hand out the front door. "I'm sorry," she whispered after them. She looked up at Siegfried, who shrugged as though he didn't know what to say either.

———

The next days were not easy ones. Try as she would, Isabella could not get the two children to like her.

The first day after her arrival, Isabella spent making a dress for Gretel from the pink cloth that the children's mother had woven before she died. All day long, while the children played outside, Isabella cut and pieced and sewed. Supper was a quiet and solemn meal, with Siegfried tired — having been out since dawn chopping wood — and with Isabella's fingers sore and needle-pricked from sewing, and with the children . . . with the children sitting there saying nothing, but only watching everything with their large, pale eyes. After supper Isabella worked by candlelight, finishing the dress just in time to present it to Gretel before bedtime.

"I don't like pink," Gretel said, though she'd seen Isabella work on the pink cloth all day.

"She's never liked pink," Hansel said.

"Children," Siegfried pleaded.

But the children turned their cold eyes on him, and he ducked his head and said no more.

"I didn't know," Isabella apologized. "I'm sorry, I didn't know."

———

The second day after her arrival, Isabella spent making a jacket for Hansel.

"Do you like this color?" she asked before she started, holding up the green cloth.

"Yes," Hansel answered as he and his sister went out to play.

But that night, after cutting and piecing and sewing, when Isabella presented him with the jacket, Hansel said, "It's wool. I don't like wool. It itches."

"No, it doesn't," Isabella said, "not if you wear it over a shirt."

"Much too itchy," Gretel said.

Their father said nothing.

The third day after her arrival, Isabella spent baking cakes as a special supper treat. While she worked, there came a tapping at the door.

"Yes?" she said to the old woman who stood there nervously twisting her cane.

"Excuse me," the woman said, squinting near-sightedly at Isabella, "but I'm your neighbor. The baker's widow. I live on the land that borders on your woods."

Isabella was about to thank her for coming over to introduce herself, but the old woman continued speaking.

"You see, it's about them children of yours. Yesterday they come and throwed stones all over my garden. I saw them just as they was walking down the last row, dropping stones as they went. It's an awful mess, and it's going to take me the better part of a week to pick up. I hate to complain, but isn't there anything you can do?"

"I'm so sorry," Isabella gasped, feeling even worse because the woman seemed so apologetic. "I had no idea. I'll send them over to clean up —"

"No," the woman hastily interrupted her. And again, "No. No need for that. I just wanted to let you know." She kept bobbing her head, almost as though bowing, as she hobbled backward with her cane. "So sorry to bother you," she said.

At supper the children ate the cakes but said they were dry and flat and that even their mother's cakes had been better.

Isabella ignored the stinging in her eyes and said, "Our neighbor has been having a problem with stones in her garden."

Hansel said, "The soil around here is very rocky."

"Perhaps so," Isabella said, not wanting to accuse them, "but she says she saw you playing there and she thinks you might have accidentally brought some of the stones in with you."

"Our neighbor is very old," Gretel said. "She doesn't know what she sees."

"And she's never liked us," Hansel added.

Isabella looked to her husband to say something. But all he said was, "Perhaps," which said nothing.

The fourth day after her arrival, Isabella stopped the children as they went out to play. "Why don't you take this cake to our neighbor?" she asked.

The children looked at each other in that way that made Isabella almost think they were talking to each other without words.

Gretel asked, "To apologize for putting stones in her garden?"

"We already told you we didn't do that," Hansel said.

Isabella said, "And I believed you," although

she didn't. "But this is simply to cheer her up about the stones, however they got there."

Hansel and Gretel looked at her with their unblinking eyes and expressionless faces. But they took the cake.

Later that morning as Isabella stood on the front stoop to shake out the dust from the rugs, she saw birds gathered on the path the children had taken. She stepped closer and saw what attracted them. It was pieces of the cake.

That evening, after the children had come home from playing and while Siegfried was still outside washing up at the water barrel by the front door, Isabella asked the children, "Did you take the cake to our neighbor as I asked you to?"

"Yes," Gretel said.

Hansel added, "She said it was dry and flat."

Isabella looked into their faces and couldn't bring herself to accuse them of lying. "Did part of the cake break off before you got there?" she asked.

"No," Hansel said.

"No," Gretel said.

Isabella had never raised children before and

wasn't sure how they were supposed to act. She tried to remember when she had been a child herself and was fairly certain she had never acted like this.

The fifth day after her arrival, Isabella woke up later than usual because she'd spent a good deal of the night crying softly. Siegfried, who'd put his arms around her but said nothing, had already left to chop wood in the forest.

When Isabella opened her eyes, the first thing she saw was Gretel standing right by the side of the bed, looking at her. Isabella shivered although it wasn't cold. "Good morning," she said, but Gretel didn't say anything.

To get away from Gretel's staring eyes, Isabella turned to get her comb from the nightstand on the other side of the bed.

And there was Hansel standing right by that side of the bed, looking at her.

"What are you doing?" Isabella asked.

It was Gretel, behind her, who answered. "We made you breakfast."

Isabella turned to look at her, and Hansel — behind her — said, "We hope you like it."

Again Isabella shivered. "Why don't the two of you go out and play?" she suggested.

Without a word, without a change of expression, the two children left the house.

The breakfast that the children had made for her was porridge. They had gathered berries for it, which spread purple stains across the pale lumps of cereal in the bowl. This was the first time the children had made any effort to do anything for her, Isabella told herself. The porridge was probably meant as an apology for the night before. And yet . . . And yet it looked too ghastly to eat.

She dumped the contents of the bowl out the door and, as the day progressed, watched the grass beneath shrivel and die.

The children had lived in the woods all their lives, Isabella told herself. Surely they should know which berries were good to eat and which were not.

But she couldn't bring herself to believe they'd intentionally try to do her harm.

That evening Siegfried came home from chopping wood before the children returned from playing. Isabella set the table and kept stirring and stirring the stew so that it wouldn't overheat and stick to the pot, but still the children did not come. "Call them," she asked of Siegfried, not daring to admit to him that they never came when she called.

Siegfried stood in the doorway and called, "Hansel! Gretel! Dinner!"

Still the children did not come.

Isabella's annoyance began to turn to worry. What if something had happened to the children? What if they didn't come home because they couldn't? One moment she thought something dreadful must have happened, the next that something dreadful *better* have happened or she was going to punish those children as they had never been punished before.

Isabella walked to the end of the front walk. "Gretel!" she called. "Hansel! Come home NOW!"

The edge of the sky faded from orange to pink to gray to black, and still the children did not come.

Siegfried took a lantern out into the woods. Isabella could see the light bobbing between the trees as he walked down to the stream; she could hear him calling and calling. He didn't come back until his voice was practically gone. "No sign of them at the stream," he whispered hoarsely; no sign of them anywhere.

They left the shutters open, with candles in the windows to guide the children home, and they left the fire in the hearth to warm the children when they came home.

But the children didn't come home.

Isabella wept loudly, telling Siegfried how she had slighted Hansel and Gretel at breakfast. Now she thought of them out alone in the woods, cold and frightened and hungry, not knowing — very obviously not knowing — which berries were good to eat and which were not.

"There, there," Siegfried said, patting her back awkwardly. "There, there."

When the sixth morning after Isabella's arrival dawned, Hansel and Gretel still had not returned.

"One of us needs to be here," Isabella told Siegfried, still hoping the children might find their own way back. "But I would like to go out to search."

The first place Isabella went was to the stream

behind the house. But even in the daylight there was no sign that the children had gone swimming there: no discarded shoes, no footprints in the muddy bank. Isabella went farther and farther into the woods, calling and calling, praying that no hungry animal nor desperate highwayman had come upon the helpless children.

She found nothing that even hinted the children might have passed by that way.

Once again at night they left the lights burning in hearth and windows, and once again the children did not come home.

At dawn of the seventh day after Isabella's arrival, Isabella started out once again. This time she headed in the opposite direction, toward the village. Surely in this direction there was not enough of the woods for the children to get lost in before they came upon the outlying houses, and from there they certainly would have been able to find their way back home. Still, Isabella thought she could enlist the help of the villagers in searching for the poor lost dears.

But before she got to the village, she got to the house of their neighbor, the baker's widow who had come to call about the stones in her garden. Smoke was pouring merrily from the chimney in the kitchen and also from the large, stone baker's oven in the front yard, and Isabella knocked at the door to inquire if the old woman had seen the children.

The door opened, and it was Gretel who stood there, with Hansel behind her, neither saying a word, both looking at her with large staring eyes.

"Gretel!" Isabella cried, throwing herself to her knees and flinging her arms around the young girl. "Hansel!" She tried to bring him into the hug, but he evaded her embrace, and Gretel squirmed away, too.

Isabella sat back on her heels. "We were so worried," she said. "You must have been so frightened, being lost."

They didn't look frightened. And they didn't say anything.

"You must have just found your way back here this morning," Isabella said.

"No," Hansel said.

"We've been here all the while," Gretel said.

Isabella couldn't see why the baker's widow would have let the children stay in her house for two long nights without letting anybody know.

She tried to see over the heads of the children into the house. There were half-eaten ginger cakes and pastry treats all over the table, crumbs tracked on the floor, tiny jelly handprints on the walls.

The old woman couldn't be home, Isabella thought. She must have gone to the village three days ago, and the children just let themselves in. But surely the old woman wouldn't have left the oven going like that. "Where is our neighbor?" Isabella asked, feeling suddenly very small and frightened.

"Right behind you," Gretel said.

"In the front yard," Hansel said.

Isabella turned around, but there was no one there, nothing there, only the oven smoking away.

And the old woman's cane, lying on the ground before it.

Isabella scrambled to her feet, telling herself that surely there was a different explanation, surely she misunderstood everything.

The children looked at her with calm, unblinking eyes.

"What have you done?" Isabella whispered.

"She didn't like us," Hansel said.

"We didn't like her," Gretel said.

"What have you done?" Isabella cried.

"Don't yell at us," Gretel said. "She was a witch."

"She was definitely a witch," Hansel agreed. "We don't like being yelled at."

"She was just a poor old woman," Isabella shouted, "half blind and half lame."

Gretel turned in the doorway to look at Hansel. Hansel nodded. They both looked at Isabella.

Isabella took a step back.

"We don't like being yelled at," Gretel said.

Isabella took another step back. Her voice shaking, she asked, "How did your mother die?"

Once again Gretel looked over her shoulder at Hansel.

Hansel said, "We don't like you."

Isabella kept on backing up until she reached the end of the walkway, then she turned and ran. Her heart pounding wildly, she ran and ran till she spotted their own cottage in the woods. She considered stopping for Siegfried but then she ran on.

After all, he was the one who had gotten her into this.

TWELVE

Evidence

If the coach turned back into a pumpkin
and the coachman into a rat
and the footmen into mice,
one can only wonder
why the glass slippers alone remained
untouched by magic's ebbing tide.

Obviously a set-up.
But by whom?

The fairy godmother's ability
didn't extend beyond midnight.
And where would a cinder girl
have ever gotten shoes like that?
Could they possibly have been a secret gift
from the stepmother,
eager to get her out of the house,
tired of her unrelenting goodness,
and beauty,
and cheerfulness
(not to mention all that singing)?

THIRTEEN

Beast and Beauty

Once upon a time, in a land where even parents had magic, a mother got so upset with her son's bad temper, sloppy clothes, messy room, and disgusting table manners that she said: "If you're going to act like a beast, you might as well look like one, too."

The next thing the poor boy knew, he had hair all over his body, his knuckles reached the floor, his teeth curved into tusks, and his nostrils were so big that anyone he stood near could see half-way up his nose.

Despite his promises never to yell again and to wash his socks at least once a week and to take out the garbage and to keep his elbows off the table, his mother would not relent. And his father *never* contradicted his mother.

"You may live alone," she said, "so that you may live however you choose."

"But Mother," Beast said — speaking quietly now, since shouting hadn't helped — "but Mother, I love you."

She continued to shoo him out the back door so the neighbors wouldn't see him. "That's nice," she said. "And you will remain a beast until you get a good and beautiful woman to agree to marry you. I love you, too," she added, and closed the door.

Now this wasn't as heartless as it sounds, for Beast's mother wasn't sending him out to beg for his food or to sleep on the hard, cold ground. The family had not one but *two* castles, the second one being deep in the woods without neighbors. It was also a magical place that would provide whatever Beast asked for, except human companionship.

Although the magic castle would have happily picked up Beast's dirty laundry and washed his dirty dishes and fixed the holes he kicked or punched into walls whenever he was angry at something, Beast very quickly mended his ways, hoping that this would please his mother and that she would allow him to return home. Besides, living out in the woods, with no friends to visit and nothing much to do beyond tending the garden, Beast had plenty of time on his hands to try to make everything perfect. Every time his parents would drop in — birthdays and holidays and the occasional unannounced surprise visit just to keep him on his toes — he would invite them to come into the house to see how clean it was. But his mother would always say, "No, no. Sitting with you in the garden is fine with me."

Then he would say, "At least let's have dinner out here so that you can see how good my table manners have become."

But she would always answer, "No, no. We ate just before we came; I couldn't possibly eat a bite more." Then she would turn to her husband and ask, "You, dear?"

And he always patted his stomach and echoed, "Not a bite more."

Then Beast would say, "Do you at least notice how neat my clothes are and how calmly I'm talking?"

"Yes, dear."

"So may I please come home?"

"Not quite yet, dear."

At which point he'd growl or kick over a lawn chair or, just to spite his mother, tear off a sleeve of his shirt.

The visit always ended with Beast pleading with his father to talk his mother into lifting the spell, and his father saying, "I'll try, but you know how your mother is."

This had gone on long enough that when, one day, Beast heard someone in his castle's courtyard, he assumed it was his parents, even though it was a freezing, rainy day. But when he went outside, he saw that it was a stranger in a dead faint on the stones. The man had obviously traveled long and hard, for he had just barely made it through Beast's gate before collapsing.

Beast carried the poor man inside, but as he was ashamed of his appearance — which he knew was somewhat alarming — he set the man down on the bed in one of the guest bedrooms, and he told the room, "Take care of the man. Provide a fire to warm him and candles so that he can see where he is when he wakes. Cover him with warm, dry blankets while he sleeps and lay out rich clothes for him to wear when he gets up."

Then Beast walked down the hallway to the dining room, calling up lights all the way. "Dining room," Beast said, "fresh tablecloth, best dishes, flowers for the center."

In the kitchen he said, "Warm and savory food on the dining-room table thirty seconds before the man gets there."

Later that evening Beast heard the man coming down the hall, calling, "Hello? Is anybody here?"

Desperate for company but afraid to be seen, Beast hid behind a half-closed door on the upper landing as the man came into the dining room.

"I say," the man said, "this is very nice." He raised his voice. "Hello. Where is everybody?"

Beast didn't answer, and of course the castle didn't answer. One of the chairs pulled away from the table invitingly, so after a while the man realized that the feast was set out for him.

Hesitantly the man sat down on the chair, which immediately pulled itself closer to the table. A fork jumped into his hand.

"Well," the man said, "thank you, whoever you are. Wherever you are."

After dinner the castle — following Beast's instructions — led the man to the library, where the man had shelves and shelves of books to choose from; and a harpsichord, should he be musically inclined; and a chess set, which played the black pieces when the man moved one of the white pawns. Beast hid behind a tapestry and watched. After two games of chess (the castle let the man win both times), several books, and a midnight snack (apparently the man was *not* musically inclined), the man yawned and stretched.

The candles in the hall lit the way back to his room, where the bed was freshly made and a silk nightshirt lay under the pillow.

Beast returned to the kitchen, where he had his own dinner, happier than he'd been in a long time. Even though he hadn't dared show himself or speak to the man, it had been good to see somebody — anybody — he wasn't related to.

The following morning Beast arranged for breakfast to be on a tray on the man's nightstand thirty seconds before he awoke.

Beast was hoping that the man would be having such a good time at the castle that he would stay. Beast was planning that, after a day or two, he would show himself to the man and the two of them would be best friends for the rest of their lives, despite Beast's unfortunate appearance.

But, after breakfast, dressed in Beast's best suit, the man called out, "Thanks for everything," and he headed outdoors.

Beast locked the gate, planning to force his visitor to stay. Still, Beast was mightily annoyed as he watched the man walk out the front door and down the front steps. But then, rather than going to the gate, the man went into the garden. And not just into the garden but *into* the garden. He stepped right on the bed of petunias. He squeezed between a rhododendron bush and some azaleas, knocking blossoms off both. He left footprints in the alyssum. And then, *then* before Beast could believe his eyes, the man reached out for and snapped off the one — the first — the only rose in Beast's garden.

Furious, Beast let out a great roar, no longer caring if the man saw him, no longer caring if the man was disgusted by him, no longer caring if the man was afraid of him. In fact, what Beast roared was, "Prepare to die," which pretty much guaranteed that the man would be afraid of him.

The man dropped the rose. "What?" he cried, looking all around. "What'd I do?" And then he saw Beast. He grew pale and sweaty, and his knees got wobbly. "I'm sorry," he said. "I didn't mean to eat your food and wear your clothes, but the castle just seemed to keep offering things to me. I thought you knew. I thought it was all right."

"I took you in," Beast cried. "I carried you in with my own hands. I gave you whatever you could possibly need or want. Did I ask for payment? Did I ask for thanks? No, I did not. All I wanted was to be your friend. But this—this is too much. How dare you go tromping through my garden to steal my rose?"

The man looked down at the rose by his feet, as though unable to comprehend that the food and shelter and clothing were free, but the flower was not. "I'm sorry," he said. "I didn't know. It's just that I was away on a long journey. I have seven daughters and each of them asked for me to bring back gold and jewels and fine trinkets. Each of them except my youngest, my Beauty. She said: 'Just come back home, Father. That's all I could ever want.' When I insisted that I wanted to bring her *some*thing, Beauty finally said, 'A rose, Father. A rose would be nice.' But my journey was not a success. My ships sank, my fortune was lost. I knew I couldn't bring back any of the things my other daughters had asked for, but I thought: 'At least I can bring back something for Beauty. Surely the mysterious host who has tended me in my illness and given me all that I could desire inside his castle, surely he wouldn't begrudge me one flower for my Beauty.' "

Beast was looking at the man skeptically. "Your daughter's name is *Beauty?*" he asked. "What kind of name is that? What did you do, call her 'Hey, you,' until she grew up, and then, when she turned out to be good-looking, you finally settled on a name for her? Or did you call her Beauty from the start, simply hoping for the best, trusting to chance that she wouldn't turn out to be a dog?"

The man was obviously taken aback. "We called her Beauty all along," he told Beast. "We hoped she'd be beautiful, and she is. Beauty is a fine virtue."

"I suppose she's lucky you didn't call her Honesty," Beast said. "That's a fine virtue, too. Or Sweet Breath. Or Mathematical Ability." But Beast was thinking. His mother had said he would stay a beast until a good and beautiful woman agreed to marry him. This man's daughter sounded like both. "I'll tell you what," Beast said. "I won't kill you—"

"Oh, thank you, thank you," the man said.

"—if you bring me back your daughter, Beauty." Actually, Beast didn't have very high hopes. What kind of man would give up his daughter to a beast just to save himself?

And, in fact, the man was saying, "Oh, no, I couldn't."

But Beast moved in closer, and after a few moments of looking up those hairy nostrils and along the length of those tusklike teeth, the man said, "Well, I could ask her."

"You do that," Beast said. "I'll give you three months. After that, one or the other of you better be here. If not, I'll come to get you."

The man finally agreed.

And three months later, he and his daughter appeared in Beast's courtyard, without Beast having to go to fetch them.

She IS beautiful, Beast thought. And the fact that she had come, putting her own life in danger to save her father's, proved that she was good, too. Or that her father hadn't told her about his agreement.

Beast decided not to take any chances and not to play any games. He went out into the courtyard right away, so that Beauty could see what she was getting into.

Ignoring the man, he said, to Beauty, "Welcome," and he took her hand to kiss it.

Beauty turned pale. She flinched as though expecting that he planned to start eating her then and there, starting with her hand and working his way up. But she did not pull her hand away. "Thank you for inviting me," she whispered.

Beautiful *and* brave.

Beast kissed her hand then. "Are my looks not to your liking?" he asked, seeing her shift her gaze away from his face.

"You look just as my father described you," Beauty said.

Ah, Beast thought, so he *had* told her. Beautiful and brave and good. "Good-bye," Beast told the man, leading Beauty by the hand into the castle, leaving the gate to show her father the way out.

It was wonderful to have Beauty for company. Although she was obviously afraid of him, she did her best not to show it. And after Beast showed her what was to be her room — furnished in fine wood and marble, decorated with silks and satins and intricately woven brocades, accented by gold and crystal fittings — after seeing all this, Beauty must have realized that he meant her no harm. When Beast bowed and said, "I will see you again this evening after dinner," she curtsied and said, much steadier than before, "Thank you."

Beast did not spy on Beauty, since that wouldn't have been polite, but he was aware of her wandering about the castle, acquainting herself with the various rooms, and the castle told him, in a delighted, shivery voice, that she seemed well pleased by what she saw.

Beast sighed with relief. He had spent days cleaning and polishing and rearranging, doing the work himself, trying to make everything perfect. At the last minute, the morning Beauty was due to arrive, he had been overcome by doubts, convinced that, because he was a beast, he had done it all wrong. He had told the castle, "You prepare for her," and the castle had told him that he'd done everything exactly the way *it* would have and that there was nothing left to do. Even that hadn't convinced Beast, but now the castle told him Beauty was well pleased.

Which made Beast well pleased.

After both their dinners (Beast ate by himself, standing up at the kitchen counter just in case his manners weren't as good as he had assured his mother, so that he wouldn't disgust Beauty), he went into the library with Beauty. Unlike her father, Beauty *was* musically inclined. She played the harpsichord for him, then they discussed music, then books, and then all manner of things.

Beautiful and brave and good and I love her, Beast thought to himself. *We get along so well. She is surely the one to break this terrible spell for me.* "Beauty," he said, interrupting her as she was reading him a poem from one of his books.

She looked up and smiled. "Beast?" she asked.

"Will you marry me?"

"Oh," she said, the smile disappearing. "Oh, no. I couldn't." And once again, as in the courtyard, she looked away from him.

"Fine," Beast said. He stood up abruptly, accidentally knocking his teacup off the coffee table. He watched the brown stain spread across the table till it dripped off the edge, onto the floor; then he swept his cup and hers and the teapot and the sugar and creamer off the table. "Fine," he repeated, and stalked out of the room.

The following morning, Beast came up to

Beauty as she sat at the dining-room table eating breakfast. His heart sank to see the flicker of fear in her eyes. "This is for you," he said, handing her a rose — there were many of them in his garden by now, but this was the most beautiful. "I'm sorry I frightened you. Always feel free to answer me honestly and from your heart. I would never harm you."

Beauty took the rose. "Thank you," she said.

But that evening, after a day of walking through the gardens and playing croquet and discussing places and things each of them hoped to see someday, when Beast asked Beauty, "Will you marry me?" she asked, "Must I?"

"It isn't a case of *must*," Beast answered. *"Will* you?"

"No," she said.

Beast didn't knock anything over, but he left the room, growling deep in his throat at the frustration, and out in the hallway he ripped a candle from its holder and chewed it to keep from shouting, *What's the matter with you?*

And so it went, from day to day. Beauty seemed to enjoy Beast's company. They would talk together and laugh together and sing songs together. But every time he asked her to marry him, she would say, "No." Some days Beast took this news better than others.

Then, one day, Beauty didn't come downstairs for breakfast. Beast had finally risked taking his meals with her, and she turned out to be very patient about reminding him not to slurp and not to speak with his mouth full, so that at this point he probably could have supped with royalty and not embarrassed his mother.

Beast went up to her room and found that the door was closed. "Beauty," he called, knocking.

"Come in," she called, but he could tell right away, even before he opened the door, that she had been crying.

"What is it? What's the matter?" he asked, trying to remember exactly how he had reacted to her previous night's refusal to marry him, and hoping that he hadn't said anything to frighten her.

"It's my father," Beauty said. "He's dying of grief for not seeing me."

"How do you know this?" Beast asked, since there had been no messenger.

"The mirror told me," Beauty explained.

"Please, Beast, please. May I go home? Just for a short while? Just to visit? Just to assure him that I'm all right?"

Beast resolved to put the mirror out in the shed. "*I* would die of grief without you," he told her.

"I'll come back," she said. "I promise. Three, four days, that's all I ask. If you let me go, when I come back, I promise to marry you."

Beast felt a brief tingle, but it wasn't enough to disperse his mother's spell. "No, I won't hold you to that promise. It must be freely given. Go, visit your father for five days. But then you must come back."

"I promise," she said. "And that's a promise freely given."

For four days Beast waited sadly but patiently for Beauty's return. Even the castle was depressed.

The fifth day Beast started to watch for her return as soon as he got up, thinking that maybe she would miss him as much as he missed her and so come back in the morning. She didn't come back in the morning, and she didn't come back in the afternoon, and she didn't come back in the evening. Beast fell asleep on the front step, still waiting for her.

The sixth day Beauty still did not return, and that night Beast howled at the moon.

The seventh day Beast decided that Beauty wasn't coming back after all, and that he really didn't care one way or the other.

The eighth day Beast went into her room and ripped the wallpaper off the walls and broke all the furniture and threw the pieces out the window.

The ninth day Beast felt all his anger drain out of him. He lay down in the garden and wept and never went back inside, not even when night came, not even when it began to rain. Beast realized that he had spoken the truth when he had told Beauty he'd die of grief without her, and he prepared to die.

The tenth day, weak and feverish, Beast thought he heard Beauty's voice. "Beast, Beast," she cried.

He didn't answer, thinking he was having a pleasant dream and not wanting to wake himself up.

But it wasn't a dream.

Beauty found him sprawled on the garden path and knelt beside him, unmindful of her gown trailing in the mud, and put his head on her lap. "Oh, Beast," she said, "I'm sorry I left you. My father needed me, and once I got there, I was sick — I thought I was dying. But then I finally realized what it was: I missed you. Oh, Beast, please ask me again to marry you."

But Beast was too weak to ask her anything. All he had the strength for was to look at her, and even that strength was failing. His eyelids began to droop.

"Then I'll ask you," Beauty said. "Oh, Beast, will you marry me?" She hugged him closer, in case he was able to whisper a reply, and her tears slipped down her cheek and fell on him. She closed her eyes, fighting back the tears. "I love you, Beast," she murmured into his hair.

Beast felt a tingle. This time it was enough. "I love you, too, Beauty," he said, recognizing that he had his old voice back, the one which came from a human-shaped mouth.

Beauty's eyes flew open. She scrambled back, letting his head fall against the slate walk with a thud. "Who are you?" she demanded. "Where's my Beast? What have you done with my Beast?"

"Beauty," the man who had been Beast said, sitting up, taking her hands in his.

She jerked them away from him.

"Beauty, it's me. I'm your Beast. I had a magic spell cast on me."

"Ha!" she cried. "A likely story!"

"It's true," he said. "Beauty, I love you. I loved you even when I kept asking you to marry me and you kept saying no."

Beauty looked closely at him. "And I'm going to say no again," she told him. "You're not the same Beast I said yes to." She remained kneeling, but she knelt tall and straight. "There," she said, "does that make you angry?"

He knew she was testing him. Beast had always had a bad temper and she was waiting to see if he did, too. "I am Beast," he assured her. "But I've changed; I've learned to control my temper. I won't get angry. I'll just lie back down here"—he stretched himself out once more on the garden path—"and continue to die of grief." He closed his eyes and folded his hands on top of his chest.

After a few moments, Beauty leaned over him. "Is it *really* you, Beast?" she asked.

"It's really me."

She sighed. "Well, then," she said, resigned, "I suppose I can love you as well in this shape as in any other."

The man who had been Beast sat up and kissed both her hands, and then he kissed her lips.

"Would you consider growing a beard?" Beauty asked.

"Anything for you, my love."

And they lived happily ever after, with frequent visits from both sets of parents, who all came *in*side the castle to see them, though Beast's mother complained frequently about his beard and about Beauty's housekeeping.